MR TRINITY'S QUEST

MR TRINITY'S QUEST

J E Stirzaker

Book Guild Publishing
Sussex, England

First published in Great Britain in 2010 by
The Book Guild Ltd
Pavilion View
19 New Road
Brighton, BN1 1UF

Typesetting in Baskerville by
SetSystems Ltd, Saffron Walden, Essex

Printed in Great Britain by
CPI Antony Rowe

A catalogue record for this book is available from
the British Library

ISBN 978 1 84624 458 2

1

I was born in a shipyard town in the north-east of England in 1945. In the early years of my life I lived with my grandparents. My grandparents were wonderful people. My grandmother was a small woman and, as I recall, very strict, though she had a warm and wonderful personality. My grandfather was a very tall man and very quiet. You could say, the strong silent type. He worked as a shipwright in the local shipyard. I can remember looking out of the window of the small terraced cottage waiting with eager anticipation for him to walk out of the shipyard gate, which you could see from the window. He would always have a toy for me in his haversack. He would walk through the front door, pick me up, and sit me on the sitting-room table. He would slip his haversack off his shoulder and say, 'Let's see what we have in my bag today,' and there I would sit quivering with excitement, waiting to see what he had hidden in his bag for me. He would pull out a toy car, give me a big hug, and say, 'Now let's have some tea.'

Everything seemed so right with me, in my own little world. Then one day, all of a sudden and without warning, the one person, my grandfather, who I thought would be there for ever, through the whole of my life, died. I knew then deep in my heart that my grandmother, a frail woman, would not be able to look after me anymore and knew it would only be a matter of time before I would have to leave this little paradise of mine.

I remember the day I left as if it were yesterday. My grandmother became ill and it looked serious. My cousin Betty, who was about eighteen, sat me on a chair by the big open range that stood in the sitting room, knelt down beside me and, with her hands over mine, her eyes filling with tears, told me my grandmother was dying. As she held me close I could hear my grandmother calling out my name. 'I'm dying,' she said over and over again and, with her voice ringing in my ears, I pulled my head closer to Betty's chest to shut out the voice crying out to me. I was very frightened and began to cry. I did not see my grandmother again and realised my own little paradise had ended.

This was how I came to be sitting on a bus staring out of the window, not knowing what was going to happen to me and what adventures would await me at journey's end. All I could think of, as tears rolled down my cheeks, was the song my grandmother would sing to me. It kept going round and round in my head. 'Little John, don't you cry, Granny's going to bake you an apple pie. We will have some for tea, a slice for you and a slice for me. Little John, don't you cry, Granny's going to bake you an apple pie . . .' It went round and round in my head. I really missed her at that moment in time.

I was brought back to reality by the sound of the bell on the bus and the conductor's loud voice shouting, 'Cottage Homes . . . last stop . . . Cottage Homes.' It was a dull rain-soaked morning as I stepped off the bus into the rain with my mother and my Aunty Becky. My mother, a small well-rounded woman with short blonde hair and a rosy complexion, was dressed in a brown skirt and white blouse with a dowdy black coat and hat that had probably seen better days. It was not my mother's fault that we had nothing. She really did try her best to clothe and feed everybody on the small amount of money she had every week.

In contrast to my mother, my aunty was a small thin woman with dark hair tied back in a bun. She was dressed in a check dress and large boots with fur round the top. A bright-blue coat and red hat with fruit round the rim. I always thought she dressed rather eccentricly. To look at them both, you would never have guessed they were sisters. As I watched the bus pull away, I waved to the conductor. He smiled and waved back. I turned, and there across the road it stood, a large grey foreboding building with large dirty windows and a large chimney that seemed to reach into the heavens. Belching out black smoke and blackening the sky as if the whole world was on fire.

We crossed the street hand in hand. I was in the middle and, as I drew closer, there in front of me stood a large wrought-iron gate with the words in gold letters: 'The Cottage Homes'. We entered through the gate and walked up along the narrow weed-covered drive. Among these weeds were bright-coloured flowers with wilting leaves. They were trying to survive, just resisting enough to add a splash of colour on such a dreary day. As I drew nearer and nearer, I could see a large figure standing in the doorway. On closer inspection, I found it to be a very large woman with a round face and bright rosy cheeks, like a clown. She had dark hair swept back off her face in waves, kept down with silver hairpins. She wore a brown dress with a large brown belt and a string of pearls round her neck.

'Good morning!' she said. 'I am Mrs Hart.' She had a quiet well-spoken voice that was very soft for such a large woman. 'You must be Mrs Carroll,' she said 'and this must be young John.' She ruffled my hair as if I was a small puppy. 'Please come in . . . Oh, do forgive my rudeness, but you must be Mrs Carroll's sister, Mrs Pescod . . . So very pleased to meet you.'

We passed through the door into a long corridor. There were doors on both sides and a long window situated at the end. When the sun peeked through this window, the rain clouds cast a long shadow off a crucifix that stood on the windowsill. This gave the corridor a haunting and eerie appearance. 'We will use this room here,' said Mrs Hart. 'Shall we have some tea while we discuss John's arrangements?' With that, she led me to a large flowery armchair in the corner of the room and gave me some comics to pass the time away. 'You sit there and look at the comics while I have a chat with your mother,' she said as she went to join my mother and auntie in another corner of the room. I couldn't help eavesdropping, as they tried to speak in hushed tones.

'Well now,' Mrs Hart said. 'I understand you wish to have John placed into care due to domestic reasons at home. I believe Mr Carroll is ill with tuberculosis and you also have a handicapped daughter Kathleen who is going to stay at a special school. This leaves the other children, three girls I believe, who will stay at home with you.' My mother nodded as Mrs Hart went on. 'I understand John is six years old next birthday in July . . . Is that so?'

'Yes' replied my mother and promptly burst into tears.

Mrs Hart and my auntie started to console her. 'Don't you worry yourself,' Mrs Hart said soothingly. 'I have some news for you that may help the situation. We have a place for John in one of our homes in Surrey. I know it's quite a long way off, but I am afraid it's the only one we have at present, so if you agree then we can get started straightaway.'

My mother lifted her head and still with tears in her eyes, she looked across the room at me and nodded her head in agreement.

'Good, that's settled then,' continued Mrs Hart. 'If you would like to come along on Tuesday next week, we will make John's travel arrangements . . . We shall give him some new clothes to travel in for the journey . . .'

I was to be bundled off to some home without one thought of how I felt. So there I was, back at mother's house, well it actually belonged to my stepfather's parents whom I did not know very well. It was a typical old pre-war terraced house with four rooms upstairs which my family lived in and four rooms downstairs which was occupied by a family whose name I think was Jones. It was a dark house but cosy with the big fire range, which made it nice and warm on dreary days. The only thing that used to frighten me was the big black beetles that they used to call black-clocks. They would only come out in the dark and when you switched the light on you could see them scurry away to the darkened parts of the room where the light did not reach. If you made the mistake of getting out of bed in the dark, you could hear them crunch under your feet, only once did I make that mistake ... The house had a long corridor with a door at either end; these were the communal front and back doors. Halfway along this corridor and situated on one side was a large narrow staircase, of which at the top were the four rooms that we shared. Three of these were bedrooms and the other room was a sitting-room-cum-kitchen, which had a view out of the window onto a cricket pitch. This belonged to the local factory and was the only bit of greenery surrounded by terraced houses and factories that continuously belched out black smoke from their chimneys. I used to sit at the window for hours on a Sunday just watching the men play. We did not have a bathroom, just a tin bath, and a toilet that was situated at the bottom of the yard that was shared by both families. No one had very much so we shared and helped each other. They all tried to make me happy but as I lay in bed that night and every one following and watched the shadows dance across the ceiling off the fire, I would cry myself to sleep thinking of my grandma and granddad, wondering what the future would hold when it was time for me to leave and travel to a strange place. To me it may as well have been the other side of the world.

Tuesday morning arrived. I stood at the bus stop with my mother waiting for the bus to arrive. It seemed like an eternity but it finally came, yet it had only been a matter of minutes. As we boarded I ran to the back of the bus and jumped onto the back seat so I could look out of the rear window at my friends and family I was leaving behind. As the bus pulled away I waved, they all began to run after the bus waving and shouting at the top of their voices, 'Goodbye!' As the bus got farther and farther away, I wondered how many of them I would see again. We arrived at the Cottage Homes after a fifteen-minute bus ride. We got off and stood in front of that long drive once again. I could see a figure in the distance. As we walked up the drive and got nearer and nearer, I could see it was Mrs Hart standing on the top step with her arms folded across her immense bosom and with a broad grin on her round face. Standing beside her was a small man with glasses that almost seemed fixed to the bridge of his nose. He had a bald head with two patches of black hair at the sides and a little black moustache. I disliked him at once and he me no doubt.

'This is Mr Smeetham,' Mrs Hart said. 'He's from the Council that runs the home that John will be travelling to this morning. First, though, we'll go into my office and fit John with some nice new clothes and discuss the travelling arrangements.'

As we walked along the corridor to Mrs Hart's office, my mind was in turmoil, trying to imagine what would happen to me when I reached the home. We entered the office and there in front of me was large table piled up with clothes.

'Now, John,' said Mrs Hart, 'we'll measure you and have you fitted out for the journey, and some extra clothes for you to change into as well. Come and see what you would like.' I looked at the clothes and thought to myself how

6

horrible they were, but how much better they were than the ones I had on. They were the usual clothes that we all wore in those days: short trousers that came past the knees, thick woollen grey socks, grey jumper and jacket. Everything was a dull lifeless colour except for the cap, which was grey, of course, but had red rings round it that made it look like a target when it was hanging on a hook. I looked at all the clothes and picked out those I wanted to travel in. Mrs Hart and Mr Smeetham packed some more in a small suitcase. 'There you are now, John,' said Mrs Hart kindly. 'There's a smart boy. You look like a real little gentleman now ... I think we'll go and have some tea and then say goodbye to your mother before you go for the train.'

We walked back to Mrs Hart's room where my mother was waiting. I opened the door and ran to her, gripped her tight and sobbed uncontrollably, saying between sobs that I didn't want to go. She cried and told me she didn't want to see me go either, but she had no choice. We hugged each other and cried and cried. It seemed like an eternity. Then a voice in the background spoke. 'Mrs Carroll,' it said. 'We must be going now or John will miss his train!' My mother broke off from our embrace.

As I left the room, I turned and looked at my mother. She was drying her eyes and smiling at me and waving. I wondered how long it would be before I would see her again. With one last look I turned and walked away.

2

I arrived at the station with Mr Smeetham. We walked up to the ticket office.

'Two tickets to Kings Cross, please . . . One single and one return,' he said in a loud booming voice, surprising coming from such a small man.

'Certainly, Sir,' replied the man behind the counter. 'Is the return for you or the boy?'

'For me,' replied Mr Smeetham sharply.

We picked up our tickets and headed for the platform. By this time, I was getting rather excited at the thought of going on a train. I had only ever seen them on posters before. As we approached the platform there she stood in all her splendour, belching out steam like some fiery dragon. And indeed that was what she was, for, there on the side of the engine in big brass letters, was written: 'THE GREEN DRAGON.' Oh, she was beautiful! I stood in awe, admiring her every feature. Suddenly a voice broke the silence: 'All aboard!' It was the guard.

'Come on, John. Let's get aboard or it will leave without us!'

After we had settled into our carriage, I pleaded with Mr Smeetham to be allowed to stand beside the window as the train pulled out of the station. After some frowning of his brow and shuffling of his feet, Mr Smeetham pulled the window down and I looked out. The guard waved his flag, blew his whistle and the train started to pull away from the platform. At first her big wheels turned slowly, but soon they got faster and faster. As we picked up speed, the steam billowed out from the funnel and from in between the wheels. The train driver blew the train's whistle – three long blasts, it was if the train was saying goodbye. Only then did I settle back in my seat and started to cry, thinking what my mother was doing and wondering if she missed me.

The journey to Kings Cross seemed to take a lifetime. Mr Smeetham didn't say much. Every time I tried to ask a question he just looked over his spectacles at me and said, 'Read your comics.' So I just looked out of the window at all the scenery as the train went first through large towns with factory chimneys belching out black smoke and then through small picturesque villages with thatched cottages, surrounded by rolling hills and sheep and cows grazing in the fields. It looked like a completely different world from the one I had left behind. And still the train went remorselessly on, never minding how *I* felt – clickity-clack, clickity-clack – a sound that, in my mind, said, 'No-going-back, no-going-back.'

We arrived at Kings Cross Station early in the afternoon, after a four-hour journey. I was rather tired but, with all the excitement of the journey and thinking of what lay ahead, the tiredness soon left me. We had an hour to wait for the next train to carry on to where we were going so we headed to the canteen for a cup of tea and an iced bun. We entered through the large swing doors where a tall thin woman with bright rosy cheeks stood dressed in a check pinafore.

'What can I get you, Sir?' she said in a funny voice, which I later found out was the way they talked in London. 'Two teas and two buns,' replied Mr Smeetham, who quickly took some change from his pocket and paid for the teas and buns. We went to a quiet corner of the canteen where we took a small table. We sat there not saying a word to each other. I sat drinking my tea and staring at the clock, waiting for the time to pass for our next train. All of a sudden over the loudspeaker a voice said, 'Will all passengers waiting for the train to Sutton on the Hill please go to Platform Four where the train will be leaving in five minutes.'

'Come along, John ... That's our train,' said Mr Smeetham.

He gulped down his tea, grabbed me by the hand and we headed for the door. Mr Smeetham moved at such a fast pace that my little legs could hardly keep up with him. We got to Platform Four just as the train was starting to move out of the station. Mr Smeetham opened a door and bundled me in. 'Phew, that was close,' he said. 'The train's leaving early. Just like British Railways, either early or late but never on time.' With that he gave a little laugh as if he had cracked some funny joke. I smiled politely, wondering what was so funny.

We sat down. 'Now, John,' he said, 'I'll explain where we are going, what it is like and whom we will meet.' But I wasn't really listening to him – after all he'd never bothered to talk to me before. So I just looked at him as if I was taking notice.

After an hour or so, we arrived at Sutton on the Hill. It was a small station with a few flower boxes dotted about here and there. As we stepped from the train, an old man came shuffling through an old wooden door towards us. He had a slightly hunched back and wore navy-blue trousers with shiny patches on the knees, a navy-blue waistcoat and a white shirt that actually looked a dirty grey colour.

'Good afternoon, Sir,' he said, taking a pocket watch from his waistcoat. He looked at it and added, 'Late again! That train's always bloody late ... Don't understand why – it always leaves Kings Cross early.' He shook his head with a puzzled look on his face. 'Ah well, never mind ... you're here now! Can I have your tickets, please?' and with those words still ringing in our ears Mr Smeetham passed him our tickets.

'Could I get a taxi to take us to Hilltop House?' Mr Smeetham asked.

'Yes,' replied the ticket collector, 'you'll find one outside the station gate.'

'Thank you,' replied Mr Smeetham, and off we went to find the taxi.

After a short walk we came upon the taxi, a large black car with black-tinted windows, Mr Smeetham knocked at the window and it slowly unwound to reveal a large black man with white hair. I jumped back in amazement – I had never seen a black man before.

'Afternoon, boss . . . Where to?' he said in a funny accent that made me smile. He smiled, too, and winked back at me.

'Could you take us to Hilltop House?' asked Mr Smeetham.

Before the taxi driver could reply we had already stepped into the taxi for the fifteen-minute ride. As we drove along, the driver, whose name was Jacob, made me laugh with his jokes, but Mr Smeetham remained stern and silent. Now and then he looked at his watch and crossed and uncrossed his legs impatiently.

As we rounded a bend in the road there it stood, a large red-brick building with large bay windows and two large chimneys on either side of the house. Pale grey smoke wafted up into the blue sky. Flowery curtains set in each window helped to brighten up the building a little and make it feel more welcoming.

We drove through the gates and there on the steps of the house stood six women in white starched uniforms with large blue belts and blue caps on their heads. As we

11

approached, they all parted and a woman in a blue uniform and blue cap came to the front. She was a small woman with dark hair and very dark eyes.

'Ah, good afternoon, Mr Smeetham,' she said.

'And the same to you, Mrs Pickersgill,' replied Mr Smeetham.

'Come now, Mr Smeetham, call me Joyce. After all, we have known each other for quite some time now . . . No need to stand on formalities. Well now,' continued Mrs Pickersgill, 'this must be young John. Come now, young John, we'll get you settled in, then we'll have tea . . . You'll stay for tea, won't you, Alf?' she added. 'That is, if you have time, of course, before your train back.'

'Oh yes,' Alf said, rubbing his hands together. 'Nothing would be more welcome.' He turned to Jacob and told him to come back in two hours for him.

'Yes, boss . . . two hours.' With a smile and a wave of his right hand at me, Jacob turned the taxi in the drive and drove off. Straightaway I missed him and his jokes!

We went up the steps of the house and through a large oak door that opened into a long hallway. There were pictures of nurses on the wall staring out at you, not one with a smile on their face. Later I found out these pictures were of previous nurses who had worked here. At the end of the long hallway was another large oak door. We entered through this door and before me was a large square room with more large doors all around the room. At the end was a large sliding door, which Mrs Pickersgill pushed back to reveal a large playground, beyond which was a large fence with tall trees behind. To the left and right were two more buildings with tall glass windows. Into one of these we now went. It was a dormitory in which all the beds were neatly laid out side by side in a large square.

'Now, John,' said Mrs Pickersgill, 'This is your bed. Put your clothes in your locker and settle down . . . You'll meet the rest of the boys after school.' (I later found out school was down the path at the side of the dormitory, through an iron gate that led to the schoolhouse behind the trees.) And then off she toddled to have her tea with Mr Smeetham. I was feeling quite hungry myself by now and couldn't wait for teatime. I remained in the empty room, sitting on the edge of that very narrow bed for what seemed an eternity. All of a sudden, however, the doors burst open and a horde of boys ran in. There must have been about forty boys in all. Then a loud booming voice shouted, 'Stop running and stand by your beds. Do as you are told or there will be no tea for any of you!'

They all stood at the bottom of their beds and there SHE stood, filling the doorway, a mountain of a woman, arms folded across her chest. She looked to one side and saw me. 'What's your name, boy?' she commanded in her loudest voice.

'J . . . john,' I stammered in a shaky voice.

'Right,' she said, 'my name is Mrs Jones, and I will tell you what all the other boys have been told: keep your nose clean.'

'It is clean, Missus,' I said.

'Don't be funny, boy, or you'll find my slipper across your backside . . . Isn't that so, young Sutherland?' she added to the boy standing at the bed next to mine.

'Yes, Mrs Jones,' he said in a trembling voice, his head bent down almost to his chest.

Now Mrs Jones clapped her hands. 'Off to the bathroom and wash your hands ready for tea, then line up in the middle of the floor.'

I followed the boys to a cold tiled bathroom off the dormitory. After we had all washed our hands and lined up, we followed Mrs Jones out of the dormitory and down the hallway with all those nurses' pictures on the wall. We turned left into another long corridor that I hadn't noticed before. We were marched through the open door and there in front of us was a long table, all laid out ready for tea. Along the walls at the back stood the other five nurses, but no sign of Mrs Pickersgill. Still busy with 'Alf', I thought.

'Right, stand by your chairs, boys!' boomed Mrs Jones and we all stood beside a chair. 'Sit, everybody.' We all pulled out our chairs in unison and sat down.

'We'll say prayers now.' Prayers? I thought to myself, I don't know any. I decided to just mumble along, though it didn't take me long to remember what I quickly learned was called 'Grace'. 'For what we are about to receive, may the Lord make us truly thankful, Amen,' chanted the boys. Almost immediately I reached out for a slice of bread. As I did so I felt a stinging slap round my ear.

'You don't do that, boy. Show him what to do, Sutherland!' Mrs Jones said and walked to the other end of he table.

Sutherland looked at me with sheepish eyes, then said in a quiet voice. 'You can't pick your bread up with your hands . . . Use your fork and put it on the side of your plate, then cut it into small pieces . . . Here, watch me do it!'

Finally, it seemed, I had found a friend at Hilltop House.

During the meal there was no sound except for everyone's jaws going up and down! I was feeling rather tired after the long journey and as soon as I had finished I got up from my chair. Suddenly Mrs Jones shouted, 'Where do you think you are going, boy? Sit down at once. If you want to leave the table, put your hand up and say, "Please may I leave the table, Miss?" Have you got that?'

'Yes, Mrs Jones,' I replied meekly.

'You may go to the dormitory and stand by your bed. I need to speak to you about the rules of the house.'

'Yes, Miss,' I replied, and with her voice ringing in my ears I left for the dormitory.

I stood by my bed shuffling my feet from side to side. I wanted to sit down on the bed but did not dare to do so in case she caught me and exacted some terrible revenge. My mind was beginning to wander when I heard her footsteps coming down the corridor. She strode into the dormitory with her arms folded and came straight for me. I took a deep breath, expecting some horrible punishment. 'Now, John,' she said in a soft voice that took me by surprise. Sadly, her words were far from being kind. There was no sympathy or concern, just a litany of rules and regulations. 'House rules. Number one: no talking after lights-out. Number two: speak when you are spoken to. Number three: no running in the corridors. As for your daily routine, you will get up at seven and go out into the playground whatever the weather – fresh air is good for you. Breakfast is at eight sharp and school is from nine until twelve, when you will have dinner. You will rest on your bed until two, when you will go back to school until four. From four to five you will go out into the playgound again. At five, we have tea and after tea is your leisure time, to do whatever you wish. At eight o'clock you will be given a mug of cocoa, then lights will go out at half past. If you are found out of bed or talking you will be punished with the slipper across your backside. Now, John, do you understand all of that?'

'Yes, Miss,' I said, although I couldn't have repeated a word she'd said.

'Good,' she replied. 'Now get your pyjamas on ready for bed. It's an early night for you as you have had a very busy day.' And with that, she turned on her heels and left me alone without even a kind word or a simple goodnight.

I got ready for bed and climbed between the sheets. I stared up at the ceiling wondering what everybody was doing back home. I began to cry quietly till at last I fell into a deep sleep.

3

The next thing I remembered was a bell ringing loudly in my ears. I opened my eyes and through a sleepy haze I saw Mrs Pickersgill swinging her arm up and down ringing a bell, and shouting at the top of her voice. 'Come on, children! Wash and put your clothes on! Wear a warm jumper – we're going out for an hour before breakfast for some fresh air. It will do you all good.' I looked at one of the dormitory windows, which were white and frosty with the cold.

As soon as everyone was ready, we all lined up in the playground and marched to the gate, and off we went down the lane. We passed field after field with nothing else in sight but cows and sheep grazing. I was feeling quite hungry by now and I thought Mrs Pickersgill would never turn us round to go back for breakfast. Finally she turned us all around and marched us back up the lane to the home. We arrived back and I looked at the large clock on the side of the building. We had been out exactly one hour. We washed our hands and then we all marched down the corridor to the hall for breakfast.

Little did I know then that this was going to be my morning routine every day for the next five years.

The days and weeks went by so slowly as if time was standing still. It was the same routine every day, watching your *p*s and *ps* just in case you said something that would offend any of the nurses. How I longed for the day when I was marched into matron's office and told I was going home. That is, if I still had a home to go to. I never received any word from home that I can ever remember. I had made some friends but sometimes I thought about running away. But where would I go to? Anyway I probably wouldn't have got very far before I was found and sent back. I never stopped feeling homesick and every day I longed for nightfall and bed when I could go to sleep and dream of wonderful adventures.

One Sunday morning I awoke with a start at the sound of Mrs Jones' bell. I never got used to it; it sounded as loud as a church bell. As usual, Mrs Pickersgill was shouting at the top of her voice. 'Rise and shine! Come on, boys, rise and shine! Get up!' I rubbed my eyes to remove the sleep from them, outstretched my arms, and yawned. Not another boring walk! And on a Sunday, too! Usually we were allowed to lie in until nine. Little did I know that on that Sunday morning life was about to change and some strange things were about to happen.

We all gathered in the playroom from which we usually started our walks. Mrs Jones, Mrs Pickersgill and all the nurses were already there.

'Right, children, sit down in a semicircle. I know it's early but there is somebody I want you to meet.'

Mrs Pickersgill turned and walked towards the door to her office. Slowly she turned the handle and said to the person on the other side, 'You can come in now.' The door slowly opened and all I could see was a large black shape standing in the doorway. As the light came in through the window the shadow came toward us, then the light hit him and there he stood, this tall thin man. He had long black hair that was tucked behind his ears. He had a thin gaunt white face and long fingernails on long bony fingers. He

17

was dressed in a long black coat with a high collar that came up to the bottom of his ears, which, if you looked closely enough, had a slight point to them.

I turned round and looked at Sutherland who sat there wide-eyed and his mouth so far open I thought it would reach the floor. He looked as if he was in a state of shock. I suppose we all were really. We were brought back to reality by Mrs Jones' booming voice: 'Boys, I want you to meet Mr Trinity. Say good morning.'

'Good morning, Mr Trinity,' we all said in unison.

'Right, off to breakfast with you now,' Mrs Pickersgill said, clapping her hands. We all stood up, still staring at Mr Trinity, and headed for our breakfasts.

As I ate my breakfast, Mr Trinity stood at the end of the table staring at me with piercing blue eyes, his hands clasped together and with a smile on his face. He suddenly turned and walked away . . . well, not exactly walked but glided across the floor, his long coat swishing from side to side. I watched until he disappeared through the door. As I ate my breakfast. I could not stop thinking of Mr Trinity and the strange way he dressed and looked. I just wondered what was in store for us because he definitely was a strange person.

After we all finished breakfast we were marched to the classroom. We all burst through the door and ran to our desks. Everybody was joking and laughing when suddenly we heard a squeaky voice come from the back of the classroom.

'Boys, boys, behave yourselves!'

It was the voice of Mrs Sweeney, our teacher. She was a little plump woman with white hair tied in a bun. She wore spectacles on the bridge of her nose and always dressed in a long brown skirt and white blouse. She always had a large brooch pinned just beneath her chin.

'Take out your books, boys, and we'll do some sums.'

No one spoke as, out of the corner of my eye, I saw this long black coat swishing from side to side. As Mr Trinity went past, his feet did not seem to make any noise. All you could hear was his coat swishing back and forth. I dug my elbow in Sutherland's ribs and pointed to Mr Trinity.

'Don't point, boy,' he said. How, I wondered, did he know I was pointing? I quickly put my hand under my desk.

Mr Trinity spun round and, as he did so, seemed to omit a glow of colours around his body. Now he began to speak, his voice echoing around the room as if it was coming from the four walls – it almost felt as if the walls were speaking to us.

'My name is Mr Trinity, as you know,' he said, his eyes darting to each of us. 'Now I know that many of you boys come from families that, through no fault of their own, have fallen on hard times. Nonetheless you have to take advantage of this moment to fulfil your dreams . . . It is up to *you* to learn! It will be hard work, but I know what all of you need to make a success of your life on this earth. With my guidance you will all fulfil your dreams, but remember that sometimes there is a price to pay for success! . . .'

With that, he walked towards the door and disappeared through it. The voice of Mrs Sweeney brought us back to reality. 'Come now, boys, take out your books and study.' I couldn't study or concentrate on anything that day. I just thought of what Mr Trinity had said and what he had meant by fulfilling our dreams.

After tea, Sutherland and I got together in the playground and decided to find out a bit more about Mr Trinity. We did not have to wait for long. We saw Mrs Pickersgill and Mr Trinity standing by the bike shed. 'Come on! This is our chance to hear what they are talking about!' We strolled across the playground and came round on the blind side of the bike shed. We listened and heard them talking. Mrs Pickersgill was asking Mr Trinity if he would like to go to the theatre that night to see a show. He replied 'yes' and arranged to meet her at eight o'clock.

We sneaked away and made a plan to sneak into his room at nine o'clock when everybody else was asleep. I couldn't wait for nine o'clock to come – I was so excited. I just lay in the darkness listening to the sounds of the night. I fell asleep only to be woken by Sutherland shaking me by the shoulders. 'Come on, John! Get ready, it's nearly nine o'clock.'

'Sorry, Sutherland, I fell asleep!' I hastily got ready and arranged my bed to look as if someone was fast asleep, just in case the night nurse came in to check on us. We headed for the big glass door off the dormitory that would lead us outside into the large garden. As we neared the door, the moon cast an eerie shadow into the dormitory. We reached the door and I looked at the night outside. I began to have second thoughts, but Sutherland grabbed my arm and led me outside into the night with only the moon to show us the way. We closed the door quietly behind us and set off across the playground to a wooden fence. We climbed over the fence which was – a forbidden act. In front of us was a gravel path and in front of that a large expanse of lawn. In the distance we saw Mr Trinity's cottage. We crossed the darkened lawn. The night was deathly silent except for the occasional hoot of a night owl. The moon cast shadows of the surrounding trees onto the lawn. The trees made eerie shadows and shapes as they swayed in the breeze. We headed for the small light that shone from the cottage window, circled round to the back of the cottage, and fought our way through the undergrowth of weeds and shrubs to the back door. We stood there taking deep breaths. I could feel the excitement building up in me, not knowing what to expect as I slowly turned the handle and opened the cottage door.

As I looked around the edge of the door, I saw a candle flickering on the table in the middle of the room. I quietly closed the door behind me. The candle on the table was flickering and casting shadows round the room. There was a small glow coming from the fireplace and, at the side of this, there was a large leather armchair. At the other end of the room stood an old wooden sideboard with a pile of books on one end. There was no other furniture to be seen in this room. There were no pictures of any description hanging on the walls. I noticed a door at the left of me and I moved slowly across towards it. I beckoned Sutherland to follow me. I slowly opened it. It was a closet.

Just as I was about to look into the closet we heard a noise outside. We looked at each other in shock, I looked round and slowly the back door began to open. Sutherland and I squeezed into the closet and, through a large crack down the panel of the door, we saw Mr Trinity enter the room. His long cloak was moving from side to side, as he walked.

We pressed our faces to the crack so we could see what Mr Trinity was up to. He walked to the table in the centre of the room. Underneath the table was a carpet. He moved the table away from the carpet and then snapped his fingers. The carpet flew into the corner of the room. I gasped in amazement and elbowed Sutherland. Sutherland elbowed me back and put his fingers to his lips as if to say, 'Be quiet!' In the same place where the carpet had been was a large circular mirror. We watched with excitement as Mr Trinity stood in the middle of the mirror and snapped his fingers once more. A big black book that had been lying on the sideboard moved from its pile and flew across the room into Mr Trinity's outstretched hands. The pages began turning repeatedly until suddenly they stopped.

Mr Trinity began to recite words from the book: 'Earth, air, fire and water, spirits of the Four Worlds, help me on my quest!' With those words he started to spin slowly round and round, and the mirror gave out a bright white light that nearly blinded us. As Mr Trinity spun round, he started to disappear into the mirror . . . All of a sudden he was gone! The carpet and the book returned to their individual places and the table drifted back into the centre of the room and placed itself over the carpet. The candle sat itself back into the centre of the table and the flame that had previously gone out burst back into life again.

We stepped out of the closet shaking, not knowing what to do. We looked at each other and then Sutherland said to me in a quaky, shaky voice, 'Shall we follow? We've got to find out where Mr Trinity has gone . . . Come on, let's do it!' His voice grew louder and louder with excitement. 'We have to do this! We have to find out!' After some debate I agreed, though rather hesitantly. We pushed the table to one side and pulled back the carpet to reveal the mirror underneath. Sutherland walked over to the sideboard and took the book from its pile. We stood in the centre of the mirror and opened it until we came to the page with the words that Mr Trinity had begun to recite previously. 'Here,' said Sutherland, 'you read them . . . I'm too scared.' He thrust the book towards me and forced it into my hands. I started to recite the words that Mr Trinity had spoken – 'Earth, air, fire, water . . .' The beam of light erupted from the mirror blotting out everything around us. We started to turn slowly. Round and round and down and down. We started to fall, flashing lights all around us, we kept on falling and tumbling until all of a sudden everything went black and we landed with a bump. As our eyes became accustomed to the dark, we could see Mr Trinity striding away into the distance.

'Where are we?' I asked, starting to become quite afraid. 'I don't know,' replied Sutherland. I could tell he was as scared as I was, as he could not seem to get his words out. 'We can't stay here! We have got to go on . . . If we lose sight of Mr Trinity we will never find out where we are and may never get back.'

We jumped to our feet and followed Mr Trinity at some distance so he could not see or hear us. We fought our way through the long grass in the shadow of the moonlight. We could see a forest in front of us as the moon came from behind the clouds, the trees bending and swaying in the wind. Mr Trinity disappeared between two large trees, their branches leaning over and intertwined to make a tunnel. We stood in the long grass a little out of breath looking down this tunnel of bent trees, their branches looking like outstretched arms.

'Well, it's now or never!' I said. 'We can't go back . . .'

After a slight pause, we looked at each other and took our first steps into the tunnel of trees. It was deathly silent, just the sound of the branches of the trees as they tried to break free from each other in the wind. I kept looking around me expecting something or someone to jump out at me. Slowly and hesitantly, we carried on walking down the tunnel until suddenly we could see a light in the distance. And there, standing in front of us, was a small cottage with round windows and a semi-circular door. The cottage had been white at one time but it was now a dirty grey in places where the paint had flaked off the walls. As we got closer, we could see Mr Trinity in the window casting a shadow on the walls from the glow of the fire that was burning brightly in the hearth. Next to Mr Trinity stood a tall man dressed in a long blue robe with a high collar that stopped just at the bottom of his pointed ears. He had long white hair and a beard that came down to his waist. On his head he had a large gold headband in the middle of which was a green jewel. On each of his long bony fingers of his hands was a ring and each ring was set with a different-coloured jewel.

As we looked through the window we heard Mr Trinity say, 'You summoned me, Master Remlin – what can I do?'

Master Remlin looked at Mr Trinity and took his hands in his and said, 'We need you! Our world and way of life are at great risk. The evil Dr Zaker has escaped from the Isle of Infinite Wisdom where he was sent to learn about his evil ways. And he is on his way back and gathering support. He already has Kaunn with him to help him, and you know he will do anything to further his cause to take over and rule. He cannot be trusted.'

I was scared. What on earth were they talking about? I turned to my friend. 'Come on, Sutherland; let's go back before we get found out.'

'We can't go back, remember! We don't know how to get back, and we need Mr Trinity. Look, we'll have to own up . . .'

We looked at each other for a few seconds and then headed for the door. We were trembling, not knowing what Mr Trinity would say or do to us.

But before we had even reached the door, a voice from the other side said: 'Come in, boys, I know you are there.'

We hesitated for a moment, and then slowly turned the handle. As we pushed the door open slowly, it creaked ominously on its hinges. We entered the room and closed the door behind us. We looked up to face Mr Trinity.

He was staring at us with his piercing blue eyes and in the semi-darkness of the room they looked like torch beams. 'I know you've been there for quite some time, boys. I can sense you and smell you from a long way off!' He lifted his head back and started to sniff the air around him. 'I smell fear!' he said. 'But don't be afraid – you are among friends.' 'Ah, Mr Remlin, these are two of the boys from the home you sent me to . . . That is Sutherland and the other boy is John.'

We both began to apologise at once, but Master Remlin held up his hand.

'Stop!' he said in a gruff voice. 'You are here now.' He clearly wasn't at all pleased. 'Come, sit down over there by the fire while I discuss with Mr Trinity what to do with you both.'

With our heads low on our chest we shuffled over to two stools by the fire and sat down, not daring to look up at either Mr Trinity or Master Remlin. 'I know it's not your fault, Mr Trinity, but it's happened and it's too late to take them back now. They might even be useful to us!' He threw us a sneering grin as he stretched out both of his hands towards us. With some force, we began to rise from the stools and flew towards him, our feet just inches off the ground. I could see the fear in Sutherland's face; it was white as a sheet! And I imagine I must have looked just the same.

4

When we got to within two feet of Master Remlin we stopped still in mid-air with our feet still off the ground. Then he spoke in that gruff voice of his. 'I can make your life unbearable,' he said, 'so unbearable you would wish that you had never been born.' His voice grew louder and louder. 'Shall we send them into the Forest of No Return and let the creatures that lurk there boil their flesh and devour every morsel before leaving their bones to bleach in the sun . . .?' He laughed menacingly.

'Please, please!' we cried, shaking from head to toe. 'Don't send us there. We'll do anything you say.'

Master Remlin scowled but lowered us gently to the ground. This was our chance to escape! I tried to run towards the door. I must have reached halfway when all of a sudden I stopped. I was still running but, when I looked down, my feet were off the ground again and my tiny legs were just moving in mid-air. I started to travel backwards towards Master Remlin.

Mr Trinity intervened: 'Boys, boys! Don't worry, we won't harm you, and we won't send you to the forest. Come and sit down and listen while Master Remlin and I talk.'

Only slightly reassured we sat down again by the fire. Master Remlin headed for a large dark-oak cupboard in the corner of the room and opened its door. He took out a crystal globe and a golden heart. He came back to the table

26

in the centre of the room and placed the two objects on the table. 'Now listen carefully to what I have to say. The Crystal Globe symbolises union with cosmic forces and celestial powers. Look into it and it will show you what dangers lie ahead. The Golden Heart will shine for ever, unless you come across anyone who say's he's a friend but is not; then its glow will cease. Use these two objects wisely and they will help you on your journey. Come now, you have to leave! Time is short. It's a long journey to where you are going and there will be many dangers along the way until you reach your destination.'

Mr Trinity headed for the door. 'Come, John, we will carry one object each.' Mr Trinity took the Crystal Globe and gave me the Golden Heart. We stepped outside and there in front of us stood three white horses.

'These are for your journey,' said Master Remlin. 'I will join you later – I have much to do before we meet again at journey's end.'

We said goodbye to Master Remlin, mounted our horses and set off on our journey towards the Forest of No Return.

'Don't be afraid, boys,' said Mr Trinity, 'keep up and don't stray from the path!'

As we got nearer and nearer to the forest, we could see eyes peering out of the trees. Strange shrieks filled the night air. Our horses started to throw their heads back and neigh constantly with fear.

Mr Trinity stretched out his arms and calmed them. 'They will be all right now,' he said. 'Remember, don't stray from the centre of the path, it's the only safe place . . .'

As we entered the forest it became pitch black. Branches swayed and cracked in the breeze, and coloured eyes peered at us from between the branches – deep red, and emerald-green, bright blue and coral pink. The creatures made noises like hungry pigs eating at a trough. I kept looking round me wondering if any of the creatures was following

27

me. Mr Trinity turned round on his horse: 'Don't be afraid! Trust me, we are safe as long as we keep to the middle of the path . . . They will not leave the trees.' I was not reassured.

Deeper and deeper we went. How I was glad Mr Trinity was with us! We rounded a bend in the path and suddenly Mr Trinity stopped. 'Right, boys, it's not far now. As we get near to the edge of the forest look straight ahead, don't look either side of you!'

'Why not?' asked Sutherland.

'If you do you will not like what you see . . . they will try to entice you in to the forest,' said Mr Trinity sternly. He took a length of cord from his cloak. 'Put this through your belts.'

We took the cord and passed it through each of our belts, joining us together.

'Right, boys, let's go, we'll gallop the rest of the way . . . Are you ready?'

'Yes!' we replied in unison.

We started to gallop towards the edge of the forest, the horses' hooves pounding into the hard ground faster and faster. It was then that I spotted the pale bones of skeletons that hung from the branches of the trees. They were the previous victims of the beasts! I froze in terror.

'Keep going!' shouted Mr Trinity. 'They are trying to get you to panic and run into the trees.'

We kept on going, our faces brushing the skeletons as we passed and making them clatter horribly. The creatures' cries grew louder and louder.

'Keep going! Keep going!' Mr Trinity kept on shouting.

It seemed like an eternity but suddenly we were out of the forest and bathed in bright moonlight. We stopped, each one of us out of breath. I looked back at the forest where creatures' eyes still peered out at us from amidst the swaying branches. Mr Trinity released the cord from our waists, rolled it up and put it back into his cloak.

'Come,' Mr Trinity said, 'there's a brook over there. We'll rest for the night and carry on with our journey in the morning.'

We settled down beside the brook and sheltered under a large overhanging rock. Mr Trinity cut some branches from some nearby shrubs and formed a windbreak either side of us. I laid myself on my back and looked up at the stars, wondering what other perils were in store for us. I must have fallen asleep because the next thing I knew was Mr Trinity's voice saying, 'Come on, boys, it's time to go.' I rubbed my eyes and opened them wide to a beautiful sunny day. Sutherland and I gathered our things together, climbed onto our horses, and set off with Mr Trinity. As we travelled along, Mr Trinity turned to us: 'You boys must be hungry. We'll stop for something to eat – there's an inn further on.'

I couldn't wait – I was starving.

Eventually we came to a small hill. As we reached the summit, there below us was a large valley with lush green fields and trees scattered about here and there. In the distance was the inn standing all by itself, smoke coming out of its chimney. We rode our horses down the hill towards the inn. As we got nearer, the smell of cooking food wafted towards me. 'Ah,' said Mr Trinity, 'that smells good. Come on!' He dug his heels into his horse and set off at a gallop.

Soon after, we pulled up at the inn, dismounted and headed for the door. Mr Trinity turned the handle and pushed the door open wide. We stood in the doorway, and there in front of us was an extremely large fireplace and over the fire was a wild boar turning on the roasting spit. It smelt delicious. We closed the door behind us and headed for a table in the corner of the room. We sat down and I slowly looked around at my surroundings. In the room, besides the three of us, were two other people, sitting in the shadows in the far corner. One of them rose from his seat and shuffled towards us, limping as he did so. He was dressed in baggy trousers tucked into large red boots, and a large black coat held together around the middle with a large red belt with a jewelled buckle. Tucked into his belt were three daggers. As he got nearer, I saw he had a thick black beard and a large earring in his left ear.

He stood in front of Mr Trinity and spoke to him in a deep voice. 'We have been waiting for you to arrive, my brother and I!' He called out to his brother to join them. I could see that he, too was limping on his left leg, and was dressed exactly as his brother, except he had an earring in his right ear.

'Sit down,' Mr Trinity said and they both sat down at opposite ends of the table. Sutherland and I looked at each other – the two men were identical, mirror images of one another!

Mr Trinity introduced us. 'Boys, I want you meet Poppy One and Poppy Two.'

I couldn't stop myself from laughing and suddenly a large hand grabbed me by the throat and said in a gruff menacing voice: 'Do you find that funny?'

My eyes were bulging out of my sockets. I managed to shake my head slightly and he let go. I was breathing heavily, trying to get air into my lungs. I looked at Sutherland, not daring to move or speak.

Then Poppy One spoke: 'Don't be afraid, boys! We're friends, and it's just that we don't like being laughed at.' They reached out and slapped us on our backs and laughed.

'These young boys, Poppies, are Sutherland and John,' Mr Trinity said. 'Unfortunately they followed me through the mirror and I can't take them back, so for now we are stuck with them both!'

'Mr Trinity,' Sutherland said in that squeaky little voice he had when he felt afraid, 'where are we, please?'

'You're in another time and world which runs parallel to yours. We can come and go between them only at full moons . . . I will tell you more later. For the moment we should eat.

Mr Trinity shouted out, 'Innkeeper, food and drink for my friends!'

How pleased I was to hear him say that! Soon the table was laden with food, with wild boar, chicken and thick slices of beef and ham, with bread and butter, and large flagons of drink. We tucked in greedily, not stopping for a minute. I just ate and ate until I could eat and drink no more.

After a while, I plucked up courage, turned to Poppy Two and rather sheepishly asked, 'So why do they call you Poppy?'

He tossed his head back and laughed. 'It's simple, my brother and I were born in a poppy field so our mother called us Poppy.'

'But why have you both got bad left legs?' asked Sutherland. 'Ah, well,' said Poppy One, 'let's say we had a run-in with Dr Zaker, and because we are twins he thought it would be rather funny for us both to have the same, shall we say, crippled legs.'

He started to go into the gory details but Mr Trinity put a hand on his arm and tapped it gently. 'Some other time perhaps, gentlemen.' Mr Trinity began to tell us more about the strange world we found ourselves in. 'Our world is called Sofala. There are many different peoples in this world just like yours. The two main peoples are the Tainos and the Uteves – we belong to the Uteves. Only a select few have the powers and magic to come and go between each world. Alas, Kaunn is one of them. You heard Mr Remlin say that Dr Zaker had escaped from the Isle of Infinite Wisdom where he had been sent to be punished for his misdeeds. He escaped with the help of a renegade Uteve called Kaunn. The isle is a large circular island surrounded by a large expanse of sea, which you can only reach by an invisible bridge. This bridge only appears every year at a full moon; somehow Dr Zaker escaped just at the time the bridge was due to appear. Dr Zaker is a Taino and very dangerous. He and Kaunn threaten to plunge our world into total darkness, and, not content with that, will go on to destroy your world also! I hope that answers your question, Sutherland!'

Mr Trinity took the Crystal Globe from beneath his coat and placed it in the centre of the table. He placed his hands over it and began to move them over its surface. After a while, he moved his hands to one side and a beam of white light erupted from the globe. In the centre of the light was a small figure dressed in white with blonde hair. To my amazement she began to speak:

'I am the Keeper of the Crystal Globe. You will meet many people on your journey. All will say they are your friends but, beware, one is your enemy! Use the Golden Heart and you will find him, but use it well! Go now, you cannot use me again until the next full moon. Heed my words!' With that, she disappeared back into the globe.

Sutherland and I sat there dumbfounded. Mr Trinity put the Globe back in his cloak. 'We'll go to our rooms now and rest until tomorrow.'

I looked out of the window and was amazed to already see the sun setting. A whole day had passed! We retired to our rooms, which Sutherland and I shared with Mr Trinity. For the first time on our journey, I felt completely safe and slept peacefully.

5

The following morning I awoke to sunlight streaming through the window. At the side of the window stood Mr Trinity, casting a long shadow across the wooden floor. He was looking out of the window not moving when all of a sudden he spoke: 'Good morning, boys,' he said, without turning round. He knew we were awake – that sixth sense he had seemed to tell him everything! He turned round and looked at us with those cold blue eyes of his. 'Come on, boys, let's have some breakfast before we leave. The two Poppies will already be having theirs.' Sutherland and I quickly got ready and went down the stairs to the most wonderful aroma of bacon cooking on the great open fire. We hurried towards the table where the two Poppies were sitting. We took our seats at the same table and tucked into the bacon and freshly cooked bread as if there was no tomorrow. While we were eating, the innkeeper came across to the table with mugs of steaming-hot, sweet tea. I tried to gulp it down but it burned the roof of my mouth.

'Take your time, young fellow,' Poppy One said. He stretched out his large hand, ruffled my hair, and gave me one of his hearty booming laughs.

After breakfast, we all sat together for a while to gather our thoughts. Mr Trinity broke the silence: 'Let's go!' We all rose from the table and headed for the door. Mr Trinity pushed the door open wide and the sun shone straight into our eyes, almost blinding us all for a second. We walked into the courtyard where our horses were, mounted them, and headed off in the direction of the sun. After a while I looked behind us and could just see the inn away in the distance. Slowly it was disappearing over the horizon until there was nothing but blue skies and green fields.

We travelled most of the day, seeing nothing and no one. It was as if we were the only people in this world. Sutherland and I began to get tired as it was getting quite late. As the sun started to set below the horizon, Mr Trinity turned to us and said, 'We will stop in half an hour so you can get some rest.' Finally, we stopped outside a small cave that would give us shelter for the night. The two Poppies gathered some wood and made a fire at the entrance to the cave. Mr Trinity took some food from a bag and we all sat down round the fire to eat our meagre rations. Mr Trinity said kindly, 'Don't worry, boys, you will have more than you can eat tomorrow! Try and get some sleep – it will be another long day again tomorrow.' Sutherland and I lay down beside the fire. I drifted into sleep to the sound of the wood crackling on the fire and Mr Trinity's voice talking to the two Poppies.

The next day I awoke to Poppy One encouraging us to get up. 'Come on, boys, time to get up!' Through half-open eyes I saw Poppy One with a huge deer wrapped round his neck. The blood was dripping down the front of his shirt and onto the ground, leaving a dark-red stain. Poppy Two came across and took the deer from Poppy One. He took it to a large rock, removed one of the large knives from his waistband, and began to butcher the deer. Every time he removed a part of the deer, he threw it onto the fire at the mouth of the cave and licked his lips. While the deer was cooking, Sutherland and I went down to a small stream at the edge of the wood and washed ourselves. By the time we had returned to the cave, the smell of the roasting deer filled the air. We all sat down and ate our fill.

After a few minutes, Mr Trinity took the Crystal Globe out of his tunic, placed it on a rock at the side of the fire, and beckoned us all to sit with him.

'But I thought you could only use it at full moon,' I said.

'We can only talk to the Keeper then, but the Globe has other uses,' Mr Trinity explained. 'It lets us see other places . . .'

He began to rub the Globe, and the mist inside started to clear and there inside the Globe we could see a figure. He was dressed in black from head to toe; he had jet-black hair tied back in a ponytail and wore a jewelled headband. Around his waist was a large green belt with a skull and crossbones, just like on a pirate flag. Over his shoulder was a bow and a quiver of arrows. From his waist at his right side hung a short sword. A large black horse was beside him and on the horse was a silver saddle and a large black shield that carried the same skull and crossbones. 'It's Dr Zaker,' Mr Trinity said.

The mist in the Globe started to clear a bit more and into view came another figure.

'Ah,' said Mr Trinity, 'that's Kaunn.'

Kaunn was dressed in a long robe just like Mr Trinity's except it was a deep blood-red with a large black belt round his waist with the same skull and crossbones on the front. 'Look,' said Mr Trinity, 'he has taken Dr Zaker's emblem. We will have to watch him closely . . . He will stop at nothing to control our world. He is just using Dr Zaker to gain control. After that, he will destroy him!'

The Crystal Globe started to cloud over and the images started to disappear. Mr Trinity picked up the Globe and put it back inside his cloak. 'Come on, douse the fire, boys, and we will be on our way.'

Sutherland and I covered the fire with soil from the cave

floor and followed Mr Trinity and the two Poppies out of the cave to the horses, which were tethered to a tree. We all mounted and set off. We rode along in silence, not looking at each other. There was no sound – no noise of birds singing in the trees or of leaves blowing in the breeze; just a deathly silence. Mr Trinity stopped and spoke in a quiet voice. 'Be on your guard. Something doesn't seem quite right.' He asked me for the Golden Heart. A golden glow shone from the centre of the heart. Mr Trinity held it in front of him and the glow began to dim. 'Be careful!' Mr Trinity told us.

The sky started to grow dark and the silence was broken by a screeching noise that made me feel very uncomfortable. It sent shivers down my spine. The noise got louder and louder and then out of the clouds came two creatures. They looked like two large birds with huge claws coming from their feet. I was amazed when, as they landed, I saw they were half man and half bird. Underneath their wings were four arms and each bird had a half-human, half-bird head with a small beak where their mouths should be. Their screeching was becoming louder and louder, as they flapped their wings in excitement and dug their clawed feet into ground. The screeching was unbearable – it went through your body, making you shake uncontrollably.

Through the noise, we heard Mr Trinity shouting: 'Dismount! Run to the trees!' We dismounted and began to run as fast as our legs would carry us towards the trees, the two Poppies bringing up the rear running just as fast as Sutherland and me even with their crippled legs dragging behind them. We reached the trees; we were all out of breath. My heart was pounding in my chest and my whole body was shaking from head to toe.

'Come,' said Mr Trinity, 'we have to get further into the forest. We should be safe there!'

The sky through the tops of the trees looked as black as

night. All we could hear was the constant noise of wings flapping and the horrible screeching. Ahead, amid the trees were some rocks.

'The rocks may give us some extra protection,' said Mr Trinity. 'Quick about it, boys!'

We crawled under the rocks and lay there not daring to say a word to each other. Above us the creatures' screeching grew louder still. I looked out from under the rock, my head just sticking out a fraction, and through the tops of the trees I could just see the wings of one of the creatures and what looked like some form of bow. All of a sudden, a shrill sound came towards us and then we heard a sudden thud as something smashed into the ground approximately two inches from my face.

It was some sort of arrow with a long shaft! It wasn't like one of those arrows you saw in a cowboy and Indian film. This one had a hook on one side, rather like a fish hook. At the other end was attached a long thin line. As one arrow came down, the one before was pulled out of the ground. Down they came one after the other, thud, thud, as they crashed into the ground. I moved closer into the small space under the rock. I could see Sutherland just a few feet from me trying to get deeper into the small opening under the rock. He was shaking all over and I could hear him sobbing.

The noise and the thud of the arrows must have become too much for him. All of a sudden, in the blink of an eye, he leapt out from under the rock and bounded towards me.

'No, go back!' I shouted as loud as I could. He was about two feet from me when, 'THUD!', an arrow embedded itself through his shoulder and into his chest. The rope tightened and Sutherland began to rise from the ground. 'HELP, HELP!' I shouted as loudly as I could. Poppy One or Two, I couldn't tell which, sprang from his hiding place. With his sword in his hand, he took one swipe at the rope and cut it in half. Sutherland's lifeless body fell to the ground with a sickening thud.

The arrows had stopped falling. I crawled from under my rock and ran towards Sutherland. I reached him and put his lifeless head into my lap. I began to cry. Up above me the shrieking noise that the creatures were making now sounded like cries of pain. Mr Trinity approached me and put his hand on my shoulder.

'Go with Poppy One now and leave young Sutherland to me.'

Poppy One led me away to where his brother was sitting. He sat me down between them both and said, 'Don't worry, Mr Trinity won't let Sutherland die.'

'But . . . but . . .' I stammered through my sobbing, '. . . he's dead . . . he's dead!'

'Watch very closely,' Poppy One said.

From beneath his cloak Mr Trinity took out the Crystal Globe and placed it on Sutherland's forehead. Next he took out a piece of silk cloth and laid it over Sutherland's body. He began to rub the Globe and a strange orange mist appeared and began to cover the whole of Sutherland's body. It swirled round him for a few minutes and then the mist started to disappear into the Globe again. As it went, the cloth over Sutherland's face began to move up and down . . . he was breathing!

I watched anxiously, my eyes wide with astonishment. I couldn't believe what I was seeing. Mr Trinity took the cloth off Sutherland. He lay there for a few seconds, opened his eyes and then sat up. I rose to my feet and walked slowly towards him not really believing what I had seen. We hugged each other – I thought I had lost my one true friend and brother.

Mr Trinity brought us back to reality and pointed upwards to the tops of the trees. I could see the creatures circling around above us. They were screaming and the noise sent shivers down my spine. They seemed to be suffering some indescribable agony. Down came crashing one of the creatures, breaking the branches from the trees as it fell. It landed at our feet, its body transfixed by hundreds of tiny silver arrows, too many to count. Another two creatures came crashing down through the trees, their faces covered in blood and their eyes staring blankly into nowhere.

Suddenly through the trees came a figure and landed in front of Mr Trinity. He was dressed in a skintight silver suit and silver boots and round his waist was a thick belt. Tucked in the belt were small pouches of small silver arrows, the same ones that protruded from the creatures lying on the ground in front of us. This strangely dressed man had long blond hair tied back in a ponytail and a silver headband. In the front of this headband were five small blue stones. When he stretched his arms out to the side I could see he had thin membranes attached from the inside of his arms down to his waist and they looked just like bat's wings.

'Hail thee, Mr Trinity,' the man said.

'Boys, this is General Giedroyc. He is the leader of the Tyrocdiles, a people of great bravery and fortitude. It will be good to have them on our side in these troubled times.'

Now down through the trees came about a hundred Tyrocdiles; one after another they came and landed on the forest floor. They were all dressed in the same manner as General Giedroyc and each one carried a small bow with a belt of arrows around their waist.

'Ah well,' Mr Trinity said to General Giedroyc, 'at least we will feast well tonight on these creatures . . . Nice fresh meat, tasty too!'

Sutherland and I screwed up our faces. 'I couldn't think of eating those . . . those ugly things, Mr Trinity!' I stammered. 'What do they call them?'

Before Mr Trinity could speak, General Giedroyc

answered. 'They are angasaurous. But Mr Trinity is right – one thing they are good for is eating.'

'But . . . but . . .' I kept on saying. Mr Trinity came over, put one arm round Sutherland and another round me and said, 'Have you tasted chicken in your world? It's just the same.'

General Giedroyc beckoned some of his men. 'There's a small clearing up ahead. We can rest for the night and feast.'

The Tyrocdiles began to tie up the bird-men and dragged them away. As we reached the beginning of the clearing, General Giedroyc waved some of his soldiers forward to make sure it was secure.

'Right,' he said, 'prepare the food! Let's have a feast.'

We lit a fire and his men began to butcher the creatures ready for the fire. When all was cooked we sat round eating our food – it really did taste like chicken. We ate and ate till our bellies were near to bursting. Mr Trinity made Sutherland and me a bed for the night from the feathers of the creatures. 'Sleep well, boys. General Giedroyc and I have some talking to do, you'll be safe now. The creatures won't be back, not while General Giedroyc's soldiers are with us!' And off he wandered to the edge of the clearing with the General.

I lay down on the feathers and soon fell asleep, oblivious to everything around me. Through the night my dreams were filled with everything that had happened these past days.

6

The next morning I woke with the sun casting shadows from the trees across my eyes. I looked around and saw everybody was already up and moving about. General Giedroyc, Mr Trinity and the two Poppies were sitting round the huge fire, eating the bird-man creature for breakfast again. Sutherland and I staggered towards the fire, rubbing the sleep from our eyes.

'Ah, good morning, boys,' said Poppy One. He had cut off some of his beard so Sutherland and I could tell them apart. 'Come sit down!'

We sat down and he gave us some creature to eat along with a cup of water. 'Drink, boys! We still have a long way to go.'

We sat by the fire, my mind wandering to home and my family, and if we had been missed and what consequences awaited us when we saw Mrs Pickersgill.

General Giedroyc broke the silence. 'Mr Trinity,' he said, 'I have to leave you now, but I will leave ten of my soldiers to accompany you on your journey.' He picked out ten of his best men.' And, with the wave of his arm, he took off with the rest of his men. As he disappeared in the distance, we heard him shout, 'We will meet again.'

Mr Trinity took out the Crystal Globe and put it down on the ground beside him. He rubbed it with his hands and the mist in the Globe began to clear. Dr Zaker was standing on a large boulder, with Kaunn beside him. Dr Zaker was waving his sword above his head as if he was already victorious. Above him circled those ugly creatures and down in the valley below was an army of such size you couldn't see the ground between them.

'Zaker has assembled an army, it seems,' said Mr Trinity in that cool unflappable voice he had. 'He has the Taino tribe with him.'

Mr Trinity put the Crystal Globe back in his cloak. 'Come,' he said, 'let's carry on. We have to meet Mr Remlin within the next five moons.' We started to march through the forest, the Tyrocdiles flanking either side of us. We kept on walking, not letting up for a minute. It must have been for hours, though I had lost track of time. Up ahead I could see the end of the forest. We got closer and closer to the edge of the trees. The sunlight started to filter through the leaves of the trees as the forest started to thin out. Mr Trinity waved at us to slow down as we got nearer to the end.

In the distance just beyond the edge of the forest I could see a figure standing motionless with both arms folded across his chest. We approached carefully as we got nearer. He was like a giant – at least fifteen feet tall. His arms were bigger than my waist. He was dressed all in red with a black cloak hanging round his large shoulders. He had no hair on his head and in between his eyes on his forehead was a tattoo that looked like a scorpion beetle.

Mr Trinity beckoned me to come to him. He took the Golden Heart from me and held it out in front of him. He started to walk very slowly towards the giant all the time holding the Golden Heart in front of him. He stopped about six feet away and the Golden Heart's glow appeared to surround him with light.

'Hail thee, giant! What is your name?' asked Mr Trinity.

The giant spoke in a loud booming voice. 'Do not be

afraid, Mr Trinity,' he said. 'Yes, I know your name . . . Your reputation goes before you. I was expecting you. my name is Alcyoneus of the Scordisi people. We wish you no harm. News travels fast. We know of your predicament and we wish to help. We are your friends.' As the giant said the word 'friend', the Golden Heart continued to glow.

Mr Trinity beckoned John again and gave him back the Golden Heart.

'Come,' the giant said, 'my village is not far away. There you can rest and eat before you carry on with your journey.'

Mr Trinity and the giant set off together and we all followed.

After a while we came to the edge of a cliff and there below us was the village. We started to walk down a steep path that wound its way down to the village. As we got nearer, we saw how enormous the houses were – the front doors must have been at least twenty feet high, the windows at least ten feet wide. People were just going about their everyday business, giving us a quizzical glance as we passed.

At the end of the village was a house that was much grander than the rest. The outside was covered with what looked like some kind of shiny metal. The giant pushed open the door and in front of us was a huge roaring fire. The heat was so intense I could feel my face glowing.

'I'll douse the fire – it will be too hot for you as you are only small,' said the giant as he tapped my head gently with his large hand. Despite his stature, the giant's touch was gentle.

In the corner of the room was a large table. We walked towards it and realised I reached only halfway up the table leg. The table was covered in food.

'Come,' the giant said, 'we shall eat first and then talk.' He lifted us up and sat us on the huge chairs that surrounded the table. 'Eat!' he said.

I couldn't believe my eyes what lay in front of me – an enormous bird with legs as big as me.

'Wh . . . what's that?' I stammered.

'Don't worry, John,' said Mr Trinity, 'it's chicken and those are apples, pears, grapes, oranges and other fruits, just like those you get back in your world, except in their world everything is larger. They have to be – as you can see, they are very large people! So tuck in!'

I took a pear, which was as big as my head. I couldn't get my mouth round it and everybody was laughing, watching me trying to eat it. The giant took a large knife from his waistband and cut it in half so I could eat it.

'Would you like some chicken as well and a nice jug of lemonade to wash it down?'

I nodded my head, as my mouth was full of pear.

We ate our fill, then Mr Trinity said, 'Come, Alcyoneus, let's talk. You have heard that Dr Zaker has escaped from the Isle of Infinite Wisdom and that the evil Kaunn is helping him to gather an army to take over our world. If he succeeds, then no one will be safe. Our world will not exist any more, and then he will be able to reach other worlds and no one will be able to stand in his way. Are you with us, Alcyoneus? We need you and your warriors – my magic alone can't beat him!' Alcyoneus hesitated for only a moment. '*I* am with you, Mr Trinity,' and he took Mr Trinity's arm in his large hand. 'But I cannot speak for the other warriors though I can try and persuade them. I will go and put your case to them.'

As they spoke, I began to look round the room. In one corner was a large shield with what looked like a scorpion carved on the front. Close by were a large bow and a sheath of arrows, and next to them stood a large sword with a blade as thick as my arm. In the other corner was a huge bed, the biggest bed I had ever seen in my life. It was at least twenty feet long and ten feet wide with large fluffy pillows and big thick blankets over the bed. The blankets reached the floor and it looked inviting. I certainly was feeling rather tired.

Alcyoneus rose from his seat. 'I will summon the rest of the warriors and see what they have to say and, if they agree, we will go with you; if not, then you are on your own.' He went round the table and helped us down from the large chairs, before heading towards the door.

We went out onto the veranda. I could see General Giedroyc's soldiers sitting round a large fire to one side of me eating their fill of chickens and drinking flagons of wine. They saw Mr Trinity and stopped; they rose to their feet and stood in silence, just looking at Alcyoneus. To the side of Alcyoneus was a large bell that he now began to ring loudly. We all put our hands over our ears to shut out the deafening noise it made. After a while, it ceased ringing and everything was deadly silent. The ground began to shake as a loud thumping noise got nearer.

I looked towards the end of the village where a cloud of dust was moving towards us at an incredible speed. It got nearer and nearer, louder and louder, until it reached the end of the village street. All of a sudden, the ground stopped shaking and the dust cloud began to clear. I could not believe my eyes – there was at least forty giants all standing there with their shields, bows, arrows and swords hanging by their sides. Each one had the same scorpion tattoo, but on their shoulder, not on their forehead. They approached in single file towards Alcyoneus. They turned and faced him, and threw their left arm across their chest in some sort of salute, just as the Romans did in the books I had read at school.

One of the giants stepped forward and said in a deep voice. 'You sent for us, Lord Alcyoneus.'

'Ah, Enceladus,' Alcyoneus said and began to explain to him what Mr Trinity had told him about Dr Zaker and Kaunn and how we needed their help to stop him.

After he had finished speaking, everything went deathly silent for a few seconds, then Alcyoneus spoke again and said, 'Are you with me?' Each of the giants looked at one another for a moment, pulled out their swords from their scabbards, raised them above their heads and shouted, 'We are, O Alcyoneus!'

'Eat and rest, then, for we have a long march ahead of us tomorrow!

With those words, the giant leader summoned us back into the house. We entered the house again through the large wooden door. I looked at the large bed in the corner with those big inviting fluffy pillows. Alcyoneus picked Sutherland and me up, one of us in each hand, and carried us to the bed. He dropped us onto those large fluffy pillows and I sank into them. The pillow came up around me as if I was some small bird surrounded by its nest away from harm. It did not take me long to fall asleep.

I awoke to find Sutherland still sleeping. I peered over the edge of my pillow and on the bed lay Poppy One and Two and Mr Trinity all fast asleep. I looked through the darkness of the room to the fire that was still burning brightly. Alcyoneus was sitting in one of the chairs beside the fire. He was hunched over warming his hands, his body casting ghostly shadows on the walls. I climbed out of my cosy pillow, got to the edge of the bed and dropped silently to the floor. I walked over slowly and quietly to Alcyoneus. His eyes were staring down onto the floor. He did not move until I reached him and put my small hand on his big brawny arm. He still did not move. He just said in a soft voice, 'Ah, young John, early riser, are we?' he said.

'I couldn't sleep very well,' I replied. 'There's so much on my mind.'

He picked me up and sat me down gently on the other chair. 'Don't worry,' he told me, 'you will be safe with us, no harm will come to you or Sutherland. We have to travel through many lands with different peoples, some good, some bad and some downright evil, but you will be safe with us. Go back to bed and try and sleep for it will be sun-up in two hours and then we will have to prepare for the journey.' He took me down from the chair and pointed towards the bed where that warm fluffy pillow beckoned me. I walked towards it and climbed onto the bed and once again nestled into the still warm pillow and fell immediately into a deep sleep.

7

I awoke to the sound of voices chattering away excitedly. I looked over to the huge table where everyone was sitting and I could smell the aroma of food cooking by the fire. I got down from the bed and wandered over to the table. 'Ah, young John,' said Alcyoneus, lifting me up with his massive muscular arms and sitting me on the chair beside him. 'Tuck in!' he said. 'Eat well for we leave in one hour.'

I looked at the food on the table. There was roast hog, bowls of fruit and bread, and flagons of wine. For Sutherland and me there were large cups filled with a red liquid which tasted a bit like strawberry. We ate and drank our fill until our bellies were practically bursting.

After finishing our meal, Alcyoneus helped Sutherland and me down. We all headed for the door and stepped into the bright sunlight where Enceladus stood with the other giant warriors and General Giedroyc's soldiers. 'Enceladus,' Alyconeus said, 'bring out their horses for them and two of the dogs.'

Enceladus beckoned to two of the giants and ordered one to bring our horses and the other to get the dogs. A lump came into my throat when I saw that the dogs were as big as small ponies! They were large grey animals with long shaggy coats, long snouts, and huge teeth. The dogs circled round everyone sniffing.

'Don't be afraid!' laughed Alcyoneus. 'They are just

getting your scent, so if you stray they will find you. They will also protect you if you get into danger. Where we are going will be dangerous; many dangers lurk round every corner.' Alcyoneus raised his arm and his warriors flanked either side of us. The dogs and Enceladus brought up the rear with Alcyoneus at the front. General Giedroyc's men took to the air flying slowly above us and off we set.

We travelled most of the day, passing through lush valleys and fields of corn, around mountains with snow-capped peaks, and alongside mighty rivers. Alcyoneus's warriors caught fish in a large net they carried, while the Tyrocdiles killed two deer.

Mr Trinity turned to Alcyoneus: 'Supper tonight, eh!'

Alcyoneus smiled and nodded his head. 'There's a small valley up ahead with a cave surrounded by rocks on both sides and a stream where we can get fresh water. We'll stop there for the night. It will be ideal – only one way in and one way out!'

We approached the end of the narrow road and there in front of us was the valley bordered by cliffs with overhanging trees. A small stream ran through the valley. Enceladus came forward with the dogs and set them off towards the cave.

'If there's anything in that cave, then they won't be in there long!' Alcyoneus said. We sat and waited. Everything was silent. The dogs came bounding back and returned to Enceladus. 'Looks like it's safe,' he said and into the valley we went. Everybody got busy. Sutherland and I began to build the fire while others skinned the deer and prepared the fish for the evening meal.

Everyone was chattering, each doing their bit to get everything ready for the meal. Suddenly the two dogs started howling and they bounded towards the entrance of the valley as a large bear-like creature came into view.

'Looks like we are in his cave,' said Alcyoneus.

The bear got on its hind legs and began to roar. The two

dogs retreated as the creature came forward growling and roaring. Then another bear came into view. We retreated further into the cave. Alcyoneus and Enceladus took some of the warriors and advanced towards them. Each of the warriors had what looked like a large club in one hand and their sword in the other. The dogs started to snap at the heels of the bear-like creatures, biting into their legs that were as thick as tree trunks. Their huge arms armed with deadly claws were swinging back and forth trying to catch the dogs. Two of General Giedroyc's soldiers took to the air and let fly a stream of arrows from their bows. One of the bears was screaming as the arrows pierced its flesh through its thick fur. It fell to the ground, striking the ground with a dull thud. Two of the giants then proceeded to finish it off with their clubs. You could hear the bones of its body breaking. It moved for a while then stopped. The other bear turned and started to make its way out of the valley pursued by the dogs and the Tyrocdiles. You could hear the growls and screams of the bear as they got fainter and fainter then ceased.

The Tyrocdiles came back into the cave with the dogs, their huge fangs dripping with blood. Alcyoneus turned to Mr Trinity. 'More meat for supper!' He snapped his large fingers on his big right hand and the soldiers started to skin the bear and carve it up. The soldiers threw the huge lumps of meat onto the fire but the dogs were given a whole leg each. They pulled the flesh to bits, greedily devouring each mouthful they took.

Later, as it got dark, the fire crackled and cast a yellow eerie glow onto the cave walls. Enceladus barked out his orders, his voice echoing off the cave walls as he gave each of his soldiers their watch-keeping duties for the night. I looked out of the cave's entrance at the full moon and the thousands of stars twinkling above in the night sky. My eyes grew heavy and I started to nod off thinking of what had happened that day.

The next day we travelled deep into the mountains. No one said anything. All we heard was the noise of the horses' hooves as they walked over the stony ground. As the sun started to go down, Alcyoneus stopped and held up an arm.

'We'll camp here for the night. We'll be safe on open ground.'

We all dismounted. A few yards away there was a small clump of bushes, and the giant warriors started to pull them from the ground to make a small ring of fires around the camp. We settled down for the night. The Tyrocdile soldiers and the giants laid out their blankets, spreading them around the campfire. Our fire was in the centre of the circle; the dogs lay down beside us.

'You and Sutherland will sleep with the dogs,' Alcyoneus said. 'Tonight they will keep you warm.' Alcyoneus started to throw huge chunks of meat onto the fire to cook. The dogs grew restless as they smelled the roasting meat. Enceladus took two large pieces out of one of the bags and threw a piece to each dog. Immediately they started to devour it, snarling and growling as they did so. We began to eat our own meat and, in the distance, we could hear the sound of wolves howling.

'Don't worry, boys,' said Mr Trinity. 'They won't come near us, even though they can smell the meat. The fires will keep them away.'

I felt apprehensive but somehow safe knowing I had the two giant dogs beside me. I ate my fill and then crawled over to where one of the dogs was lying. I lay down beside it and snuggled into its fur. The warmth of the fur and heat of the fire soon made me fall asleep.

*

I was in a deep sleep dreaming of home again when I was awoken by the howling of the wolves. They sounded quite near. I looked towards the firelight. Through the flames, you could just see the wolves through the circle of fires pacing up and down, too frightened to come inside. Alcyoneus's men formed a circle with the giants around Mr Trinity, the two Poppies, Sutherland and me. The giants drew out their large swords, the Tyrocdiles their bows.

'They're waiting for the fires to dim,' said Mr Trinity. 'We have no wood left to keep them going; they'll attack when the fires get low.'

The wolves were getting more and more agitated. One by one the fires started to go out. 'Get ready!' shouted Alcyoneus.

A howl went through the air piercing the night sky and breaking the silence of the night. The first wolf leapt towards us over a dead fire, its fangs oozing saliva, but as it did so it began to change. 'Geynies!' shouted Alcyoneus, his voice booming into the night sky. With one swipe of his sword he took the creature's head from its body and it flew into the air and landed at Mr Trinity's feet, its red eyes staring up at us. The two dogs snatched it away and started to tear at the flesh.

The other Geynies started to leap over the smouldering fires, there bodies transforming before our eyes. They became transparent – you could see the bones through the skin and the veins running through every inch of their flesh. They were howling and screaming, as the giants slashed out with their swords and the Tyrocdiles fired their arrows. You could hear the bones breaking and with every one that fell to the ground you could hear its screams running through the night air, sending shivers down every inch of your spine.

On they came, one after the other, as the slaughter went

on. Alcyoneus circled round everyone, shouting, 'Don't break the circle! Keep it together!' One of the Geynies leapt over the circle, landed in front of us, and advanced towards the two Poppies. They drew their swords and stood in front of Mr Trinity, Sutherland and me. Just as it began its assault, the two giant dogs leapt from either side towards it and buried their teeth deep into its bony flesh. It fell to the ground and the dogs started to tear at its long sinewy body, ripping off bits of flesh and bone and crushing it with their powerful jaws before devouring it. I turned away and buried my head into Mr Trinity's cloak so I couldn't see what was going on around me. All I could hear were the screams of the Geynies as they fell around us.

Only as the morning light began to come over the horizon did everything finally fall silent. I turned around and looked at the carnage before me. Geynie bodies were lying all around; some with arrows protruding from their scrawny torsos, others with heads missing where the giants had decapitated them with their swords. Enceladus strode forward, raised his blood-soaked sword and let out a scream of victory.

'Burn them!' shouted Alcyoneus. 'Send their spirits back to the land of the Geynies where the fires of hell will consume their scrawny remains for eternity!'

'Burn them! Burn them!' everyone was shouting.

They dragged the carcasses into a blood-soaked pile. Alcyoneus picked a smouldering ember from the fire and blew gently on it until it was bright red. The soldiers gathered some kindling that lay on the ground around us and covered the bodies with it. Alcyoneus placed the ember onto the pyre and it burst into flames. We all stood and watched as the flames and smoke billowed into the early morning light.

'Come,' said Mr Trinity, 'we must carry on.' We mounted

our horses and set off. After a while I looked back, watching the smoke rising into the morning sky, and wondered if we would ever get back to our school or normal way of life.

'Look in the distance, boys. Before you are the mountains of Thodulf. We have to cross them to reach the Flatlands of Sondron,' Mr Trinity told us.

As we got closer, I could see the snow-topped peaks disappearing into the white clouds. After travelling most of the day, we came across a small oasis at the foot of one of the mountains.

'We shall rest here for the night,' said Alcyoneus. 'We have water and enough wood to make a fire. Tomorrow we cross the mountains. It will be a long journey and a cold one!' That night Sutherland and I lay down beside the dogs and snuggled into their fur. I could see Mr Trinity take the Crystal Globe from under his cloak. He placed it on the ground in front of him and I could hear his voice very softly talking to the others around him. 'Look,' I could hear him say, 'it's Dr Zaker. He's gathering more men around him, if you can call them that!'

'He must have gathered at least five thousand! We have to find more soldiers,' I heard Alcyoneus say.

'I know,' Mr Trinity said. 'We have to move quickly and cross the mountains to the Flatlands. We should be able to recruit the soldiers we need there. At least then we will have a chance of defeating Dr Zaker. We *have* to succeed . . . We all know the consequences if we don't! Master Remlin has travelled to the Lands of Magorig where the Ice People live to ask their leader to help our cause . . .'

I heard no more. I had fallen fast asleep, weary from our endless days of travelling.

The following morning, I awoke and looked up at the mountain in front of me. Its peak looked higher and higher, reaching into the white fluffy clouds. At the base of the first mountain a path led upwards until it disappeared into the clouds.

'Come,' said Alcyoneus, 'let's climb.' Everyone formed a single line and we started to climb higher and higher up the narrow mountain path. I looked down and the ground fell away into the distance. Alcyoneus beckoned us towards him.

'Here, tie this rope around your waists.'

When we had done as he said, he tied the other end to his waist. We had only gone a few more yards when the ground started to shake beneath us.

'Hug the mountain!' shouted Alcyoneus. We all put our backs against the cold cliff face as huge boulders started to fly past, narrowly missing us. The horses started to get nervous and they began to stamp their hooves on the narrow path. One reared up and tried to turn; instead, it fell over the edge and went tumbling down, over and over, until it disappeared somewhere far below.

The whole mountain was shaking with a thunderous noise and then, as quickly as it had started, it finished. Everything fell silent. No one spoke. We were all just trying to get our breath back. In front of us the clouds parted and a craggy face appeared in the side of the mountain. A deep booming voice rang out like thunder echoing all around the mountains.

'Who dares to cross the Mountains of Thodulf? Speak, for I am the guardian of the mountains . . . SPEAK!'

Mr Trinity stepped forward. 'I am Mr Trinity of the Uteves people and we need to cross the mountains to the Flatlands of Sondron.'

Mr Trinity began to explain why we had to cross the mountains. The Guardian of the Mountain listened to Mr Trinity and after a short silence he spoke.

'Mr Trinity, I have heard of you, I know of your quest. You are an honourable man and your cause is just. You may pass in safety.'

'Thank you, Guardian!' said Mr Trinity.

A mouth appeared in the craggy face of the mountain.

'How do we cross?' I said to Poppy One and Two.

'Watch!' they said.

Mr Trinity stood on the ledge of the mountain, stretched out his long bony fingers, and said in a loud voice, 'We are ready, Guardian of the Mountain, to cross.'

We all stood there in silence. The mouth opened and a stone tongue rolled out towards us like a bridge, making a thunderous creaking noise.

'Come!' said Mr Trinity. 'Let's cross. Just keep on walking and don't look down.'

We all started to cross one by one onto the tongue that led into the large mouth on the other side. We all crossed safely and entered the mouth.

I heard a rumble that got louder and louder. We turned round and watched as the tongue rolled back into the mouth of the mountain and disappeared, leaving nothing but a blank wall behind us. We were inside the bowels of the mountain.

'Come,' said Mr Trinity, 'follow me!' We set off into the darkness. My eyes quickly grew accustomed to the darkness, and I could see in front of me a narrow path. Down it went until I could see it no more. As we went on, we saw on either side of us deep veins of some bright silvery lines. I touched them and ran my hand across them.

'Yes, John,' Mr Trinity said, 'it's pure silver! Don't touch it.'

'But can't I take a piece?' I replied.

'No!' he said gruffly. 'We are guests of the Guardian of the Mountain. He would not be very happy if we abused his hospitality. Come, we have to hurry – time is of the essence.'

We travelled down the path for what seemed like hours. Finally, I saw a light at the end of the path. As we got closer, the bright sunlight began to come through the opening. The end of the path opened onto a large ledge. We all stood there and looked out onto the Flatlands of Sondron.

8

As we looked down across the Flatlands, I could see people moving about in the fields and cottages with smoke coming from the chimneys. We proceeded to make our way down the winding path that would lead us to the Flatlands of Sondron. As we descended, I could see that the people in the fields were all men; I could not see any women at all.

In the distance, a cloud of dust began to get nearer and nearer. We reached the bottom of the path at the edge of the mountain just as the cloud of dust came to a halt. As it cleared, we saw sitting on two black horses the most beautiful women I had seen. They were small in stature, with short-cropped blonde hair and very deep-blue eyes. They were dressed in black short halter-tops with leather trousers and boots. Each one had a bow over her shoulder with a quiver of arrows across her back. Round each of their tiny waists they wore a leather belt that carried a short sword and a dagger.

One of the warrior women rode forward. 'I am Christinos, leader of the tribe of Sondros of the Flatlands of Sondron. Speak! Who are you and why do you come to our land?' Mr Trinity began to explain our situation and who we were and the need to gather all the help we could along the way to defeat Dr Zaker and put him back where he belonged. 'I have heard of you, Mr Trinity . . ., of you and your friends. You have gathered together a fearsome force but even you cannot defeat Dr Zaker. However, come! You must be hungry and weary. Follow me!' Christinos said.

The women turned and set off at a slow pace, with us bringing up the rear. We passed the men working in the fields who looked up and saluted Christinos as she went by each one then returned to their work. As we entered the village other woman warriors started to leave their homes. Each house was round with a pointed roof and a small chimney that belched out smoke into the blue sky. Each roundhouse had a small door and on either side of this was a small round window. We headed for a large roundhouse at the end of the village, surrounded by a large moat and reached by a wooden bridge.

We reached the edge of the moat and dismounted. Christinos clapped her hands and two men ran forward and took our horses. 'Take them and feed and water them!' As Christinos and the other woman dismounted, another woman warrior strode forward.

'This is Judithos, my second-in-command. Come, Mr Trinity,' Christinos said, 'we will eat and talk.' She clapped her hands again and two more men came forward. 'Take Alcyoneus's men and General Giedroyc's Tyrocdiles, and feed them well.'

The men bowed and Christinos then rose and beckoned us to follow her. Mr Trinity, the two Poppies, Alcyoneus and Enceladus (who were too tall and had to shuffle into the roundhouse on their knees) and Sutherland and I followed behind Christinos and Judithos into the roundhouse. Inside was a large fire in the centre of a circular room. A table stood at one side of the fire, underneath a small round window. At the other side of the room was a bed. Two men were putting large plates of food and drink onto the table.

We all sat at the table and ate greedily until we could eat no more. No one said a word; all you could hear were people's teeth chomping on the sides of beef and gulping down large flagons of drink. We ate and ate until the table was bare of food. Christinos beckoned the two men forward and they cleared the table.

'Now,' said Christinos, 'what can we do for you, Mr Trinity?' Her voice was soft but firm.

Mr Trinity took the Crystal Globe from his cloak and placed it on the table in front of him. He placed his hands over it and began to move his long bony fingers across its surface. The mist in the Globe began to clear.

'Look, Christinos,' Mr Trinity said. We all stared at the Globe and there was Dr Zaker, astride a jet-black horse, his long red robe hanging over his shoulders and resting on his horse's back. In his right hand he held his large sword and in front of him stood the strangest army I had ever seen. The soldiers did not look very tall, about five feet, but had large thickset bodies. They did not have feet as such, but large talons at the end of each so-called toe. Their heads were half human and half bird. They had long beaks and each beak was fitted with razor-like teeth. Their eyes were bright red and bloodshot with blue veins running through them, which were set deep into their heads. Each one was carrying a sword and a dagger in their 'hands', which you couldn't see as each was covered in a kind of glove.

Christinos slammed her hand onto the table, which made the Globe shake. Her eyes grew wider with a look I had never ever seen before, a look of sheer hatred. Her mouth began to quiver and her voice changed from soft to fierce, with a touch of fear and a dryness in her throat. 'Silvienes!' she said over and over again, slamming her tiny hand down on the table. Every time she said the name, Mr Trinity grabbed her arm and looked into her eyes. All of a sudden calm came over her.

'Sit,' he said, 'Sit! Be calm!' Mr Trinity sensed something was wrong. 'Tell me, Christinos, tell me!'

She began to tell Mr Trinity how as a child her family was captured by these creatures. She was made to watch while they ate them alive. My throat began to become suddenly very dry. Mr Trinity took hold of her hand and said, 'You know what I'm going to ask you,' and she said, 'Yes. You want us to help you in your quest to fight these creatures.'

'You know, Christinos, if we don't do this your lands and all the other lands will be overrun. Dr Zaker and Kaunn will take over and our world will never be the same. It will become an evil world of fear and darkness, and it won't just be our world.' Mr Trinity glanced at Sutherland and me.

Christinos looked at Mr Trinity with her blue eyes. 'You have my help – I want revenge! Come, sleep,' she went on. 'Tomorrow will be a busy day. Rest now.' The men started to lay straw beds on the floor for us to sleep upon. I lay down beside the fire and slept. Once more I began to dream of home.

The next morning I awoke to the early-morning sun streaming through the round window straight into my eyes. I could smell the aroma of meat cooking on the open fire. I shook Sutherland.

'Come on!' I said. 'Breakfast!'

We crawled over to the fire. The Poppies grabbed both of us by the collar, sat us down by the fire and cut off a large piece of meat for each of us, thrusting it into our hands. They slapped us on the back. 'Eat, boys!'

Everybody was eating heartily. I couldn't take my eyes off Christinos – she was beautiful. Poppy One brought me back to reality as he bent and whispered in my ear, 'You're too young!' After we had all ate our fill, Christinos and Judithos arose and said, 'Come, we have a long way to go!' We all stepped outside. I couldn't believe my eyes – there on horseback were the most beautiful women I had ever seen, except in books. There must have been at least a thousand of them, all of them on horses of dappled grey. They were dressed in the same black-leather top and trousers, and a black-leather helmet decorated with silver studs and a large deep-red plume. Each one had a crossbow slung over her slender back and a sword by her side.

Judithos galloped to the front of the female warriors, raised her sword above her head, and shouted, 'Christinos, Christinos!' All the other warriors withdrew their swords, their blades glinting in the morning sun, and started to shout their leader's name over and over. After a while, Christinos raised her hands and everybody went silent.

'Warriors of Sondron, our friends need our help.' She went on to explain Mr Trinity's quest. 'We will be going into the unknown to fight your worst enemy, the Silvienes! Are you with me? Many of your families have suffered at the hands of these creatures and now we can have our revenge. Are you with me?' she shouted again.

'Christinos! Christinos!' they shouted. 'We are!'

Everyone fell silent. A man appeared and Christinos beckoned him forward with her hand. He shuffled forward on his thin bony legs with his thin arms folded in front of him, his head bowed over his chest. He had a grey beard and grey hair tied back in a ponytail.

'This is Honitos,' Christinos said, 'He is the overseer of the men and he will pick twenty men to accompany us. They will wait on us. They will hunt for food and do all the carrying and cooking.'

Honitos moved towards Mr Trinity. 'Pleased to meet you, sir. I have heard great stories of you and your deeds of great courage. I am your servant!'

As he got closer, the Golden Heart, which I had attached to my belt, began to glow dim.

'Mr Trinity!' I said.

Mr Trinity put his arm on my shoulder. 'I know, I have seen! Don't worry.'

Christinos summoned Honitos to gather the men and horses and food for the journey. 'We will give you one hour before we leave. Go now!' she commanded.

Honitos turned and scurried away.

Mr Trinity turned to Christinos. 'Let's walk for a while and discuss our plans before we leave.' Off they both went, walking side by side.

Alcyoneus nudged me in the shoulder. 'Don't they make a lovely couple?' He smiled and everybody started to laugh.

We turned and went back into the roundhouse and sat beside the fire to wait for their return. I told everyone about the Golden Heart I carried and what it was for. 'Don't worry!' Poppy Two said. 'Mr Trinity can take care of himself!'

9

An hour later everything was ready and Mr Trinity's army was ready to depart. It was an awesome sight – all the Sondron warriors, their helmets shining in the bright sunlight; Alcyoneus's giant soldiers standing in two columns with Enceladus at the head with the two giant dogs; General Giedroyc's men circling above us, the sunlight shimmering on their silvery uniforms, casting rainbow colours all around us. Mr Trinity told me that the different materials in their uniforms gave off different colours – blues, reds, yellows and dark golds – and that it quite dazzled the enemy if they looked at them for too long.

Honitos approached Christinos, his head slightly bowed. 'The horses are ready, my Queen.'

'Good!' she replied. 'We will leave now. Have you got everything you need for the journey?'

'Yes, my Queen. Ten wagons full of food and wine, enough for four days' journey.'

'Excellent,' she replied.

Mr Trinity touched Christinos's arm. 'I don't want to sound like I'm having a moan, but will that be enough?'

'Yes,' she replied. 'We can hunt on the way, too. There will be plenty of game. These are just the basic things we need to get us to the lands of Gawen.'

The horses were brought forward for us to mount. Poppy One and Poppy Two took Sutherland and me and put us on the huge horses. Everyone mounted their horses except the giants; they would have to walk, as there were no horses big enough for them. General Giedroyc's men would fly ahead to the next campsite. Finally, when everyone was ready, off we set.

Everybody rode in silence. All you could hear was the noise of the horses' hooves and wheels of the wagons as they went over the hard stony ground. On and on and on we rode, the sun getting hotter and hotter. As the day went on, Poppy One passed me some water. 'Drink, for it will be a while before we reach camp and settle down for the night.' I couldn't wait. I was hungry and beginning to feel a little tired. We rode on as the sun became lower in the sky, like a big red fireball.

Just as the sun was about to disappear over the horizon, we stopped. Judithos, who rode at the front, galloped back towards us.

'We will stop here for the night.'

I was relieved. I don't think I could have gone on much longer as I was getting really tired. I looked over at Sutherland who was also nearly asleep in his saddle. Just as Sutherland was about to fall off his horse Poppy Two grabbed him by the back of his coat and gently lowered him to the ground.

'There's a stream ahead where we will stop for the night and rest,' said Christinos. 'Three more days and we will enter the land of the Gawen peoples.'

I dismounted and, taking the reins of my horse and Sutherland's, I led them towards the stream for them to drink. Poppy Two had Sutherland over his shoulder and headed towards the stream with me. Once there I let go of the horses and collapsed in a heap on the ground. Poppy Two dropped Sutherland into the cold water which instantly woke him up. The next thing I knew my head was being thrust into the cold stream. I was trying to get my breath as I came back out of the water, which was so cold it woke me up immediately.

'Feeling better, boys?' asked Mr Trinity. 'Come, let's sit by the fire.'

Honitos and the other men had been busy setting up a large campfire. We shuffled over and began to dry our wet heads. I was extremely hungry and watched as one of the Sondron men threw something into the fire. It looked like some weird creature that you would find in my *Dan Dare* outer space comics that I read back home. I did not care what it looked like; I just wanted something to eat, and it smelt good as it slowly cooked over the big open fire.

At last, one of the Sondron men came forward with the weird-looking creature on a round iron plate. I stared at it for what seemed like minutes, just looking at it from every angle. I picked it up, held it to my nose, and started to smell the cooked carcass. A voice next to me whispered in my ear. 'Eat, eat!' It was Poppy One. 'Come on, eat! You will be surprised when you taste it.'

I took a bite and started to chew. I *was* surprised. It tasted delicious. I began to eat faster. A large hand tapped me on the shoulder: 'Slow down, slow down!'

I turned to Poppy One and said, 'It's just like chicken.' And he laughed out loud in that bellowing voice he had.

I licked every piece of meat from my fingers, took a large swig of water and lay back. My stomach was full to bursting. I looked up at the stars and drifted off into a deep sleep.

I awoke the next morning to the sound of everybody dismantling the campfires. Christinos, Judithos and the other Sondron women were getting their horses ready for the journey. Everyone was very busy with his or her own duties. Honitos came towards us, his scrawny body hunched over, his hands clasped together twiddling his long bony fingers.

'Is they're anything you would like, young sirs?' he asked in that cringing voice he had.

'Be off with you!' Poppy Two said gruffly.

Honitos scuttled away bowing as he went.

'Don't trust him,' Poppy Two said to Poppy One. 'He's a shifty creature – we'll have to keep an eye on him!'

We got onto our horses and sat and watched as the Sondron men packed everything into the wagons, doused the fires, and finally saddled their own horses. Alcyoneus raised his arm and then everybody got in line and off we set. The giants were at the front with the dogs, while today Christinos rode beside Mr Trinity and us. 'I think we should cross the Quaking Grounds to the land of the Gawen peoples,' Christinos said. 'It will shorten our journey by two days.' I didn't like the sound of that and turned to Sutherland. We looked at each other and we both shrugged our shoulders.

We set off just as the sun was starting to rise in the morning sky. It was already beginning to get hot. It would be quite a while to the next campsite and I kept on wondering what to expect when we got to the Quaking Grounds. In the distance we could see some large birds circling overhead. Alcyoneus, the chief of the Scordisis, motioned us to stop. He summoned Enceladus. 'Take two men with you, and see what lies ahead.'

The three giants rapidly disappeared over a brow of the hill that lay in front of us, their long legs taking one stride to about six of ours. It was not long before a figure appeared on top of the hill and beckoned us forward. Everyone broke into a gallop. We all reached the top of the hill and looked down into a crater below us. There on the ground was what appeared like small people lying all over the bottom of the crater. Their tiny bodies were broken and covered in blood. The birds were pecking at some of them, tearing the flesh from their tiny torsos. Christinos with some of her warriors galloped down into the crater and started to chase the birds away from the bodies.

General Giedroyc's men began to circle round the birds up above and with their small bows began to shoot them from the sky. As they fell to the ground, the Sondron men raced into the crater and began to gather them up.

Poppy One turned to me and with a grin on his face said, 'Bird again for supper tonight! Ah well, better than nothing.' The thought of it turned my stomach; after all, they had just been eating these tiny people.

Mr Trinity turned to Alcyoneus. 'I think we should check for survivors and bury the rest. We can't have any of the night animals feasting on them.'

Judithos took some of her warriors and began searching amongst the broken tiny bodies, while some of the Sondron men dug a pit to bury the bodies.

Alcyoneus bent down and picked up a tiny figure in his large hand. Holding it gently, he started to walk towards Mr Trinity. We all got down from our horses and waited as he climbed to the top of the hill where we waited.

'Sit down, Mr Trinity,' said Sutherland, and I sat along-side the two Poppies. Alcyoneus bent down and placed the tiny figure on the ground in front of Mr Trinity. It was a female, about eighteen inches tall and dressed in a pale-blue tunic, blue tights and dark-blue ankle boots. She was dark-skinned with dark-brown spiky hair. Gold earrings hung from her pointed ears. She lay on her back in front of Mr Trinity, not moving.

'I think she's still alive,' Alcyoneus said to Mr Trinity. 'Can you do anything?'

Mr Trinity took the Crystal Globe from his cloak and placed it beside her tiny head. He took the same piece of cloth that he had used to cover Sutherland's body and placed it over her. It began to glow just as it did with Sutherland. Her tiny hand started to move and then her other hand. Mr Trinity took the cloth and the Crystal Globe and placed them back in his cloak. The tiny body started to sit up. Then, all of a sudden, she leapt into the air and started to hover in front of Mr Trinity. She opened her eyes; they were the bluest eyes I had ever seen. Then I spotted the small wings on her back – I couldn't believe what I was seeing. She was a fairy. I looked at Sutherland and saw the astonishment on his face.

She settled onto the ground in front of Mr Trinity. 'Thank you, kind sir, thank you! I am forever in your debt.'

'What is your name fairy?' Mr Trinity replied gently.

'My name,' she replied, 'is Fairy Nough.'

I let out a loud laugh, and Poppy One slapped me round the back of the head. 'Show some respect, young John!' Fairy Nough flew towards me in a flash: I didn't even see her move. She hovered about six inches from my face, leant forward and said in a small squeaky voice. 'If you make fun of me again I will turn you into a toad, young man.' And then, in an instant, she flew back towards Mr Trinity and settled back onto the ground.

'I'm sorry,' she replied.

'It's all right,' Mr Trinity said. 'It will keep him on his toes. Besides, I don't think he will make a good toad. Tell me what happened.' Fairy Nough wiped a small teardrop from her cheek and began to tell us her story. They had been on their way from their land, Siphonos. 'It's a small island in the land of the Gawen peoples surrounded by a large lake. The leader of the Gawen, General Dylantos, doesn't bother us. He even helps us now and then when we run short of things we need – after all we're a small people! . . . We were on our way to Magorig to attend the wedding of Queen Lindis and King Gandelin who, as you know, are extremely rich people . . . but that's another story . . .'

We all sat listening as she continued: 'We had stopped for a rest and thought we would be safe, but suddenly, from

out of the sun, came those dreadful vulture-like birds . . .
They just swept down on us! We didn't stand a chance. We
had no weapons to protect ourselves. There was too many
and they just picked us off one by one. I lay on the ground
and played dead, hoping they would leave after they had
had their fill. I was lucky you came across me before they
had their chance to get to me. Thank you, Mr Trinity!'

She started to sob tiny tears. Poppy Two took a cloth
from his pocket, ripped it in half, and began to wipe the
tears away. Everyone just sat there in silence, not knowing
what to say. Mr Trinity broke the silence. 'You're safe with
us now. We're on our way to the lands of the Gawen
peoples. You can come with us, if you like. We'll take you
to your home.'

'Thank you,' she replied, 'but I have to reach Queen
Lindis and King Gandelin to tell them the bad news.

'Don't worry,' Mr Trinity said. 'I will send two of General
Giedroyc's men to explain everything to them.' He called
over two of the soldiers and explained to them what they
had to do. 'Yes, Mr Trinity,' they said and turned on their
heels and flew into the air.

'They will get there before you will,' Mr Trinity
explained. 'Eat and drink for we have a few more hours of
travelling till we reach the Quaking Grounds.'

Alcyoneus came back and reported to Mr Trinity that
they had buried the small people in a deep grave.

'Come, boys,' said Mr Trinity. 'Let's be on our way.' Off
we set down into the valley past the tiny grave marked with
a simple cross, on which was carved the words.

HERE LIE MANY FRIENDS

The two Poppies broke into song, trying to cheer everyone up. On we travelled, the two Poppies still singing the
same old song. I couldn't understand a word and it was

getting monotonous. I just wished they would be quiet. Suddenly there was silence. My wish seemed to have come true; it was pure bliss. I turned round and there they were still singing but no sound came from their lips. I turned back to the front and straight ahead facing me and sitting on the rear of Mr Trinity's saddle was Fairy Nough with a grin on her tiny elf face. I looked at her and she smiled back.

Bliss, pure bliss, I thought. All I could hear was the sound of the horses as they walked over the ground. I turned to my right and there was Sutherland lying on his saddle sound asleep. He had strapped himself on somehow with a piece of rope. I thought, *Why not?* I lay down across the front of my saddle and nodded off to the swaying movement of my horse.

Some time later someone nudged me. It was Poppy Two. I rubbed my eyes and looked around. The sun was starting to disappear on the horizon, like a big ball of red fire. I looked in front of me and there were the Sondron men busily making the camp for the night. A fire was already blazing and a large animal like a boar was turning on a spit. I looked forward to another scrumptious meal. And it wasn't long before, with a full belly, I snuggled into the thick bushy fur of the Scordisi dogs and drifting off into a deep sleep.

10

The next morning when I awoke I saw Sutherland was already awake and hastily saddling his horse with one of the Sondron men.

'Come on, young John,' said Mr Trinity. 'Hurry to it. Another long day today.'

I picked up my saddle, ran to my horse and started to saddle it quickly so I would not hold everyone up.

'It's about an hour's journey to the Quaking Grounds,' Mr Trinity continued. 'Honitos and the wagons have already left earlier so they wouldn't hold us up.'

When everybody was in their place, off we set. The giants led the way with Christinos on one side and Judithos on the other. General Giedroyc's men were, as normal, flying just above us. The two Poppies were at the rear and Fairy Nough was sitting on the back of Mr Trinity's saddle. We rode along under the hot sun. In the distance, though, dark clouds were gathering in the sky with the odd bolt of lightning flashing through them.

'Let's hope the rain keeps at bay,' said Mr Trinity. 'We really do not want to be caught in a downpour.'

At last we reached the edge of the Quaking Grounds.

'Everyone dismount!' shouted Christinos. 'From now on we will have to lead our horses. It will take a day to cross the Quaking Grounds. Follow in Alcyoneus's and Encela- dus's footsteps in single file.'

Ahead of us was a narrow path that led through the middle of the Quaking Grounds.

'Stick to this path whatever you do, and whatever happens *do not* step off of it,' Christinos warned. 'This is the only solid piece of ground through the Quaking Grounds!'

We all started to move along the path, and I could see the ground either side of us moving up and down in a wave-like motion, making a rumbling noise as it did so. The horses' ears started to prick up and their nostrils twitched. Two of the giants who were at the rear of the column took Sutherland and me and placed us on their shoulders, while two more took our horses to lead them along the path.

The ground shook and rumbled with every movement, and as the ground opened up in places, you could see the remains of broken wagons and the bleached bones of horses and people who had panicked and strayed from the path. It made me all the more determined to hang on to the giant whose shoulders I was on.

On we went, deeper and deeper into the Quaking Grounds. The black clouds above us were getting darker and darker and there were bolts of lightning flashing everywhere. Sutherland's horse started to panic and rear up. The giant soldier was using all his strength to try to calm the animal down when, all of a sudden, a large clap of thunder rumbled across the dark sky. The heavens opened and the rain came down, soaking the Quaking Grounds. Sutherland's horse was still panicking and rearing. Above the thunder Mr Trinity shouted to the giant, 'Let it go!' The giant let go of the reins and the horse reared up on its hind legs and jumped away from the path. The waterlogged ground now looked like waves on the sea and the horse seemed to be swallowed up by them!

The rain got heavier. 'We have to get out of this soon,' Mr Trinity shouted. 'The path will disappear under this rain if it doesn't stop soon!'

Alcyoneus seemed unfazed. 'Everyone keep tight together,' he boomed, 'and hold the hand of the person in front of you and don't let go!' By now the path had flooded and the water came up to everyone's ankles. Even General Giedroyc's men had difficulty staying in the air. Two of them were struck by lightning, their bodies falling from the sky into the Quaking Grounds, never to be seen again.

As suddenly as the rain had started it stopped. Soon all that was left of the rain were small puddles on the path. The dark clouds disappeared and the sun came out. It shone down on the wet ground and started to dry it, the steam rising into the air and forming a fine white mist that quickly evaporated into the atmosphere. The Quaking Grounds were still moving either side of the path but we carried on walking.

Suddenly one of the giants ahead of us cried out and pointed. There on the Quaking Grounds was what remained of some of the wagons that Honitos had started out with earlier that day, all smashed to pieces with some of the Sondron men. As we all stood and watched, the broken wagons and the dead men began to disappear into the ground until there was nothing left, just the ground moving up and down as before.

On we marched for the rest of the day, and at length we saw, at the foot of a hill ahead of us, Honitos and what remained of the Sondron men setting up camp. The sorry tale of what had happened was soon told. Some of the wagons had overturned in the storm and some of the Sondron men had panicked. We were all glad we had arrived safely and settled down to eat the hearty meal that Honitos had prepared. No one was saying anything; we just kept gorging ourselves on the food. After everyone had finished, Mr Trinity spoke.

'Over that hill is the land of the Gawen peoples. In the morning we will send an emissary to their leader, General

Dylantos, and ask him to meet us to discuss the problem we have with Dr Zaker. Until then I think we should all get a good night's rest and worry about tomorrow when it comes.'

We all settled down for the night. I lay down and looked up at the stars. Soon I was in a deep sleep.

The next thing I knew was Sutherland kicking the sole of my shoe. 'Come on, John, time to get up!' I wonder what these Gawen people are like? Can't wait!' he said.

'They could be head-hunters,' I said, annoyed at being woken like that, 'and eat people like us!'

He swallowed and gulped. 'Do you think so?'

Poppy One smiled. 'Don't worry, young Sutherland! You have nothing to worry about. They don't eat small boys, not enough meat on them!' With those words he turned on his heels and headed towards Mr Trinity.

Sutherland looked at me, his eyes wide.

'He's probably just joking,' I said, 'you should know what he's like by now.' We got up and strode across to where Mr Trinity was sitting with the two Poppies.

'Good morning, boys. Slept well, I hope? Sit down and have some breakfast.' There was a large flat pan sitting on top of the smouldering fire with what looked like eggs. They were white with a deep-red yolk in the middle.

'Grab some bread,' Poppy Two said. 'Help yourself, Sutherland.'

I looked at Sutherland, then looked at the pan, then looked back at Sutherland again.

'It's all right. They are eggs, just *our* eggs, but they taste the same as the ones from your chickens.'

Reassured, we both grabbed a large chunk of bread and tucked into the eggs, the red yolk running down the sides of our chin. We couldn't eat fast enough. We sat by the fire watching the burning embers slowly dying, the smoke billowing into the air.

Christinos and Judithos came over and sat down next to Mr Trinity.

'I've sent a giant herald ahead to see General Dylantos,' Christinos said, 'to ask if he will see us, or at least let us pass through his land. We will just have to wait until he comes back.'

We sat there watching the fire going out. The sun was high in the sky now, beating down fiercely on my back and soaking my tunic with sweat. It seemed as if hours had passed when a shout from one of the giant guards jolted me back to reality. He was pointing to the crest of the hill. I looked round. At the top, along the ridge, was a line of about one hundred men and in the middle of them a big round man. I couldn't see what he looked like as the sun was in my eyes.

The herald we had sent came running down the hill towards us. He stopped, his chest heaving up and down as he tried to get his breath back.

'Calm, calm!' said Mr Trinity. 'Tell me.'

We all expected to hear the worst. We all heaved a sigh of relief as he said through short breaths that the General would see Mr Trinity. Mr Trinity nodded his head, and the herald turned and waved his arm in a beckoning motion.

The large round man started to walk down the hill, his soldiers on either side of him in a long thin line. As he advanced, I could see he was about six feet four, with a large red beard and red shoulder-length hair. He wore red pantaloons, a brown sleeveless leather jacket over a red shirt, brown knee-length boots and a large black belt about six inches wide. Tucked into this were four daggers and hanging from his waist was a sheathed sword. His soldiers were dressed in skintight red trousers with the same sleeveless leather waistcoat. Each one had a headband round his head to keep the hair from falling into his face. Their arms and chests were adorned with tattoos, and each carried a sword hung over his shoulder and a dagger strapped to each leg.

As they got nearer I started to back away but Mr Trinity grabbed my arm and pulled me back. 'Don't be afraid! Give me the Heart.'

I had forgotten about that. I passed it to Mr Trinity who held it in the palm of his hand. It started to glow and, as General Dylantos got nearer, it kept on glowing. Mr Trinity passed it back to me and I put it back in my tunic.

General Dylantos stopped in front of Mr Trinity and held out his hand. Mr Trinity took his hand.

'So pleased to meet you,' General Dylantos said through his large bushy beard. His bright blue eyes twinkled. 'I see you have quite a formidable force with you. Tell me what I can do for you,' he added.

Mr Trinity started to tell the story about Dr Zaker and the evil Kaunn and how everyone had become part of this band of warriors. General Dylantos kept on nodding his head as Mr Trinity told him of the consequences that would befall this land if Dr Zaker defeated us.

After Mr Trinity had finished, everyone sat silent for a while, then General Dylantos spoke in a deep croaky voice.

'I understand,' he said. 'I've heard of this Dr Zaker . . . Not a very nice person by all accounts . . . How can I help you?' he said.

Mr Trinity looked at him, took the Crystal Globe from his cloak and sat it on the ground. 'Look into it!' Mr Trinity said.

General Dylantos started to look into the Globe. As the mist cleared, there was Dr Zaker with Kaunn marching up and down in front of his weird army. Almost at once the Globe started to cloud over and Mr Trinity picked it up and put it back in his cloak.

The General was obviously disturbed. 'We will help!' He took Mr Trinity's hand and added, 'We won't let you down.'

They sat for a while chatting about the plans they should make. 'Come,' said General Dylantos, 'I think we should leave now. We should get to my village about nightfall. There we can celebrate our peoples being as one.'

Mr Trinity raised his hand as if to silence General Dylantos. 'Sorry for interrupting' he said, 'but I think we should wait till the defeat of Dr Zaker and Kaunn before we celebrate properly . . . maybe just a little tipple.'

General Dylantos nodded and smiled. 'You're right, of course,' he said. He rose to his feet and took Mr Trinity's bony hand. 'Come, friend,' he said and helped Mr Trinity to his feet.

Mr Trinity waved to Alcyoneus and the other leaders of the different peoples. 'You lead the way, General, and we'll follow you.'

We all set off and started to climb the hill that would lead us to the land of the Gawen peoples. Sutherland and I couldn't wait. We bounded up to the top of the hill racing each other as we went. We reached the top together and looked down on a wide valley filled with tall trees like conifers, fields of golden long grass and a river as blue as the sky. In the distance rose a mighty range of snow-capped mountains! Deer drank from the water's edge and curious spouts of water spurted droplets of water into the sky, creating dazzling rainbows. These, General Dylantos later told me, were small volcanic geysers.

Everybody reached the top of the hill and looked in awe at the landscape below.

'Beautiful, eh!' said General Dylantos. Mr Trinity just nodded. A voice next to me broke the silence, 'Come, John, you and Sutherland can share this horse.' It was Poppy One. He picked us up and sat us on the horse. General Dylantos signalled to his men and off we set, descending the hill to the valley below. Everyone got into single file as we walked along the path beside the river. The long golden grass on the right-hand side of us swayed gently in the breeze. Every so often a small geyser would spout tepid water into the air which would drift across, dampening our clothes and cooling us down.

11

The mountains grew nearer, their snow-covered tips disappearing into the white clouds. The path in front of us started to widen out as we came to a bend in the river. As we turned, there in front of us was the Gawen village, though it was big enough to be called a town. Dotted all over the flat plain were square huts with straw roofs, small windows and a door at the front. Each house had a small garden where vegetables grew. Around the village was a large moat about twenty feet wide, with one bridge in front of us and another on the far side leading to a great expanse of forest. The river entered the moat and flowed around the village then back into the river to disappear into the mountainside.

'Here we are, Mr Trinity – welcome to the village of Gawen,' said General Dylantos. 'What do you think?'

'Very impressive,' replied Mr Trinity, 'and well fortified too.'

'Ah, you can't be too careful,' the General said, 'the Cannibals have their village in the Forest of Parek. We don't venture there and we don't bother them, and usually they don't bother us. But you never know, it could all change one day . . . Still, let's not dwell on that,' he added. 'Come, let's eat and be merry for tonight and worry tomorrow!'

General Dylantos smiled at all of us, waved his hand in the air and everybody started to cross the wooden bridge. Once everyone was over, General Dylantos summoned Christinos. 'Tell your men to take the far end of the village near the bridge and set up camp for themselves. I'll post guards on the far bridge, just in case there *is* any trouble . . . you and the rest of your leaders will be guests in my house.'

Off we set to a large house by the river's edge, overshadowed by the towering mountains that lay behind. The sky was darkening and the snow-covered tips sent flashes of reflected moonlight across the river. As we neared, I could see the smoke coming from a chimney that poked through the straw roof. The smoke ascended into the night sky like some ghostly apparition. The windows emitted a yellow glow, as if the whole of the inside of the house was on fire. The front door began to open slowly, creaking on its large black hinges. The glow from the fire looked warm and inviting.

General Dylantos explained that it could get very cold during the night. 'Just like the deserts in your world,' he said.

'Have you been to our world?' I interrupted.

Mr Trinity looked at me with those piercing blue eyes and put his long bony finger to his lips as if to say, 'Silence'. 'I'm sorry!' I replied. 'I was ju . . . just curious.' I said, the words coming out of my mouth in a nervous stammer.

'It's all right, Mr Trinity,' said the General. 'Not to worry . . . Come.' He put his arms around our shoulders and we headed towards the open door. We entered the house and I looked aorund. On one side of the room was a large bed. It must have been at least fifteen feet wide. On the bed were large cushions and pillows and big thick coloured blankets.

General Dylantos turned to me. 'This is where we all sleep . . . Everyone in the same bed. Best that way, everyone keeps warm snuggled together!'

On the other side of the room was a large oblong table, covered with all kinds of fruit, vegetables and meats.

'Come, let's eat. Take your fill and forget about tomorrow,' the General said, raising his glass.

We were all about to tuck in when the door opened. There, silhouetted in the open door against the night sky, was Christinos. I stared at her for a moment, taking in her beauty . . . A clip to the back of my head brought me back to reality.

'Tongue in, young John,' Poppy One said. 'You'll have to grow a bit first!' Everyone laughed and I could feel my face starting to burn with embarrassment.

'Come in, everyone,' General Dylantos said. In came Christinos followed by Judithos with Alcyoneus and Enceladus shuffling forward on their knees as they were too big to stand in the room. 'Everyone settled for the night then?' asked General Dylantos. Christinos spoke up: 'Everyone is settled. Guards posted on each bridge and everybody is content as they have a full belly and a roaring fire for the night.'

'Good, good,' General Dylantos said. 'Come, eat and sit by the fire with Mr Trinity and me. Forget about our troubles for a while.'

I watched Alcyoneus and Enceladus tuck into a huge leg of what looked like pork, though, in their hands, it looked about the size of a turkey drumstick. Fairy Nough just flew up and down the table picking up bits of fruit and the odd piece of bread to chew. We sat there for about an hour just eating and drinking and not saying a word, as if this was going to be our last meal for some considerable time.

At last General Dylantos spoke: 'I think young John and Sutherland should rest now while we discuss the coming days ahead.' With a wave of his hand he gestured to the bed in the corner.

Sutherland was only too happy to head for the bed, but I wanted to stay and listen to the leaders' plans. I lay on the bed with the pillows all around me and watched as two of

General Dylantos's men cleared away the table and Mr Trinity took the Crystal Globe from his cloak and placed it on the table. I was determined to take a look. I turned to Sutherland to say, 'Come on, let's get closer,' but he was already fast asleep. I sneaked off the bed and began to crawl towards the table. As I got nearer I could see the Keeper of the Globe appear and start to speak to Mr Trinity . . . I strained to hear what she was saying.

Just as I was about to get a bit closer, a large hand came down and caught me by my belt buckle. I was lifted up then thrown towards the bed. I landed face down into the pillows. A huge bellowing voice said across the room, 'SLEEP!' It was the giant Alcyoneus. Frustrated, I lay down on the bed and watched as they listened to what the Keeper of the Globe had to say. I would just have to imagine everything! Besides, Mr Trinity would probably tell us in the morning anyway. I turned and snuggled into the blankets and fell asleep and dreamt of home.

I do not know how long I slept, but I awoke to the crackling of the logs in the fireplace. I could not move as everyone was on the bed. I squeezed out of the pile of sleeping bodies, all, it seemed, making horrible grunting and snoring noises. I sat up, looked around me in the now dimming firelight, and saw the giants Alcyoneus and Enceladus stretched out in front of the fire. At the table sat the solitary figure of Mr Trinity staring intently into the Globe, which was still in front of him. I got nearer and nearer and he still did not move. I climbed onto the chair and reached out for the Globe.

I had just put my hand on it when all of a sudden a long bony hand grabbed me by the wrist and wrenched it away. I looked up at Mr Trinity. His eyes were blank. The Globe started to glow with a bright-red colour and a stream of smoke started to pour from the Globe and rise up towards the ceiling. Frightened, I took my hand from Mr Trinity's grasp and ran back to the bed. I got in between Poppy One and Two and watched, with my mouth wide open with astonishment.

The smoke circled around above Mr Trinity and began to disappear into his open mouth. In it went as if he was inhaling the smoke from a cigarette. All of a sudden, his body gave a jolt as if he had received an electric shock. He rose swiftly from his seat and started to move his body, shaking his shoulders and arms, and moving his head in a circular motion. After a few minutes he picked up the Globe and headed towards the bed, I buried my head in a pillow and pretended to be asleep. All I felt was the bed move as Mr Trinity lay down next to me. He reached across and touched my shoulder.

'Young John,' he said, 'don't be afraid by what you saw, but promise me you won't tell anyone, will you?'

'I promise!' I replied.

He turned his head to one side and soon fell into a deep sleep. I lay awake just thinking of what I had seen and then I, too, drifted off into sleep.

I awoke the next morning to a smell like rotten eggs; the whole room stank with the aroma. Then General Dylantos let off a sound from his lower regions – flatulence! The two Poppies followed this with a fart in unison. I smiled to myself and thought, *They even do that together!* I jumped off the bed and ran to the door with Sutherland hot on my heels. We reached the door and threw it back wide, the door creaking on its hinges. We stood there taking in deep breaths, filling our lungs with fresh air.

An hour later, when everyone had got up, we gathered at the camp near the furthest bridge. All the fires had been doused and the last of the smoke was rising into the now blue sky as the sun was just coming over the horizon. *Another hot day*, I thought. Mr Trinity and the other leaders sat in a circle discussing the next phase of the journey. General Dylantos wanted to incorporate the Cannibals from the Forest of Parek into our now growing army.

'Well, I for one don't fancy waking up one morning,' interrupted Poppy One, 'and finding myself in some pot!'

Mr Trinity smiled. 'Come now, Poppy. It won't be that bad; they might just want to take an arm or one of your fat legs.'

Everyone started to laugh.

'Well, I'll be all, right,' chipped in Fairy Nough, 'not much meat on me!' She giggled as she hovered in front of Poppy One and smiled one of her impish grins.

'So are we agreed then?' said General Dylantos.

Everyone put their hands up in agreement but I knew the two Poppies were not quite so sure.

Soon after; everyone went to pack for the journey. I seized the chance to ask Mr Trinity where we were going next.

'To the land of the Volsci people,' he explained. 'They are the most ancient of all the peoples of Sofala.'

'And what are they like?' I asked.

'They are as peace-loving as the rest of us – or most of us, I should say,' Mr Trinity said. 'All these centuries we have lived peacefully, helping each other if and when needed, everyone abiding by the same rules that were laid down all those centuries ago. Nobody tried to inflict their beliefs on anyone, not like your world! And that is precisely why we have lived so harmoniously . . . Still, that's another story!'

Honitos and the Sondron men had already left the camp and were moving off across the bridge towards the island of Siphonos where Fairy Nough came from. Christinos had told them to wait at the edge of the Inland Sea and set up camp for the night, as it was a good day's march for us all before reaching the island. First, though, we had to go to the Forest of Parek. Sutherland and I were not too happy. After a hour or so we reached the edge of a dark, brooding pine forest.

'You stay here,' General Dylantos said. 'I and my two men will make contact with the Cannibal leader, Hipictu. Would you like to accompany us, Mr Trinity?'

Mr Trinity nodded. 'Good, then let's go,' and off they went at a steady trot.

At the very edge of the forest they dismounted. General Dylantos strode forward about another fifty feet, withdrew his sword and the daggers around his belt and placed them on the ground in front of him. He raised his hands and placed them round his lips like a megaphone and shouted, 'Hipictu, it is I, General Dylantos. I wish to speak to you.' He lowered his hands to his side and waited.

The branches in the trees started to move and out into the open stepped a pygmy, his dark body covered in a chalky substance. He wore a gold necklace around his neck and large gold earrings dangled from each ear. He had a gold bone through his nostrils and gold nipple rings adorned each breast. On his head was a feathered head-dress and the lower part of his body was covered with a patterned loincloth. Around his neck he carried a blowpipe and a small pouch of arrows hung at his side. In his right hand was a wide curved sword.

He lifted his left hand and about twenty more pygmies stepped from the trees. I swallowed and gulped, my throat going dry thinking that soon I could be on an open fire turning on a spit for their next meal!

Hipictu lowered his left hand and put his weapons on the ground. The warriors who had come out of the trees stepped back into the thick undergrowth that surrounded the trees. Hipictu began to stride forward towards General Dylantos and General Dylantos towards Hipictu.

They sat down on the grass, both with their legs crossed. General Dylantos started to talk, making sign language with his hands. They must have sat there for an hour talking to each other. At the end they both nodded and rose to their feet. Hipictu turned and disappeared into the forest. General Dylantos picked up his weapons, mounted his horse, and, with Mr Trinity, headed back towards where we were all sitting, waiting with bated breath.

General Dylantos started to speak in his deep voice that seemed to crackle as he spoke as if he was trying to clear his throat all the time.

'Well,' he said, 'they *are* prepared to help us . . .'

Alcyoneus interrupted. 'There must be a catch. What do they want in return?' he boomed.

'Ah, well, that's the problem. I had to promise him that if they took prisoners during our campaign . . . well . . . they could eat them!'

I couldn't stop myself from gasping. This, though, was a war and we needed to have every advantage we could.

'If they do want to join us,' the General continued, 'I told them to meet us at the edge of the Inland Sea opposite the island of Siphonos. Now quickly, we don't want to stay near this place any longer than we have to. The Cannibals prey on unsuspecting travellers who stray too close to the edge of the forest . . . A lot of people have disappeared into that place.'

We mounted our horses and galloped off into the setting sun. Alcyoneus was running alongside us, his long legs striding out and pounding the ground, making it shake with each step. As we galloped away, we heard the shrieks of something or someone calling out in pain. It sent shivers down my spine. 'Looks like some poor soul is on the menu tonight,' General Dylantos said.

But even that couldn't put me off thinking of my next meal . . .

12

That night I had been asleep for quite some time when I heard a tiny voice whispering in my left ear.

'John, John! Wake up!'

It was Fairy Nough. She was sitting on my chest a few inches from my face. 'Would you like to see my home before you travel tomorrow?' she asked in her tiny squeaky like voice. 'Come!' she said.

I rose from my bed. The whole camp was silent except for the one or two guards patrolling the outer perimeter, marching up and down while everyone else snored.

Soon we came to the edge of the Inland Sea where a tiny boat was moored. In the distance was an island. You could just see its shape in the moonlight as it shone through the moving clouds. 'Get in!' said Fairy Nough.

'It's too small,' I pointed out.

'Put your foot in.' she told me.

I did as she told me and, as if by magic, I started to shrink! Soon I was the same size as Fairy Nough. Even my clothes had shrunk to fit.

She pushed the boat off from the side and it steered itself across the calm sea. There were just the ripples on the water as the boat crossed to the island of Siphonos, Fairy Nough's homeland.

'You are very privileged to see this,' commented Fairy

Nough said. 'It's just my way of saying thanks, but don't tell anyone, will you, it's our secret.'

As we got closer, I could see hundreds of small lights shining from the trees, and soon I realised what I had thought to be toadstools were houses. At the stem of each 'toadstool' was a small door and, above, lights shone from a row of little windows. As we neared the jetty, lots of fairies gathered, waving to Fairy Nough. And as we disembarked, they parted and a fairy appeared dressed head toe in blue. He had long blond hair hanging over his shoulders, and on his head was a silver headband with a blue jewel in the centre. Beside him was a woman dressed in a long white gown. She had dark spiky hair just like Fairy Nough's. Both wore golden sandals encrusted with different-coloured jewels.

Fairy Nough said, 'John, these are my parents – King Ronough and Queen Melia . . .' We stepped closer. 'Father, Mother, this is John. He is with Mr Trinity and the others who saved me from those terrible creatures.'

'We will be forever in your debt,' said the King. 'I have heard of this Mr Trinity . . . a great man by all accounts. I can't wait to meet him but that will have to wait till morning. Please come with me, young man. Let me show you my home before you go back.'

We strode from the jetty onto what looked like a pave-ment slab, only just big enough for us all to get onto it. When we were all safely in position, it started to move, the ground below us started to disappear and we began to float higher and higher. Soon we were above the trees and there in front of me, perched on the side of a mountain, was a magnificent castle, except it was in the shape of a giant toadstool. There were even spotted battlements and an arched drawbridge. As we got nearer, the drawbridge began to open. Now the slab stopped and we all stepped off onto the drawbridge and headed through an opening into a large courtyard surrounded by what looked like solid rock. As I looked closer, I saw there were windows all round the courtyard filled with coloured glass, each depicting the portrait of a man and a woman. King Ronough explained to me that they were the fairy kings and queens who had gone before them.

As we walked through the courtyard bathed in the bright moonlight, an arched-shaped door opened before us. We stepped through the door onto another large slab of stone, and this too started to rise just like an elevator in a hotel. I looked up and saw a bright light above. Nearer and nearer it got until we finally arrived at the top. I stepped off onto a marble floor. I couldn't believe my eyes – the walls were made of what looked like gold with a silver border going round the room studded with multicoloured jewels, all neatly arranged in various patterns and shapes.

At one end of the room stood a huge marble fireplace, and on either side a large tiger sat, looking out across the room, through deep-red jewelled eyes. A fire was blazing away in the fireplace, the light from the fire bouncing off the jewels and gold walls. I looked up above me and the ceiling was the same as the walls – gold encrusted with jewels. In the middle of the room was a large marble table with golden legs and six gold chairs encrusted with jewels and diamonds. The table was laden with all kinds of fruit and vegetables. At one side of the room was a large window. I walked across to it and looked out – the clouds were just above me, all white and fluffy just like the quilt on a bed. I looked through the glass across the tops of the trees and down into the valley below where the toadstool chimneys were emitting little puffs of smoke into the night sky. I looked down and saw the lights in the windows start to go out one by one. It was magical!

I turned round and looked around me, my mouth still

wide with amazement. 'I see you are impressed, young John,' said King Ronough. 'Yes, all this is real, but watch closely!' He waved his hand in front of him and for a moment the whole room changed. Everything – walls, table, chairs – was just dull plain wood. I gasped, and the King laughed. He waved his hand again and the room returned to its former spendour.

'Come,' he said, 'let's eat for soon you will have to leave and go back to Mr Trinity, and continue your quest.'

After a delicious meal, the King spoke again. 'It is time for you to go. My daughter will take you back, but you must not tell anyone what you have seen in this room.'

'I won't say a word,' I told him, 'but why did you bring *me* here and no one else?'

'I think my daughter has taken quite a liking for you, but don't worry! You can only ever be friends – you can't stay that size for ever.'

Secretly I was quite relieved.

'I have something for you,' the King continued. He got up from the table and walked across to a small door in the wall. He opened it and took out a small round glass ball like a marble. He put it in the palm of my hand. 'Don't lose it,' he said. 'This will protect you and Sutherland, but only use it if you really need it and are in extreme danger.'

'But how?' I asked.

'You will know when the time comes,' King Ronough said with a smile.

With those final words, Fairy Nough took my hand and led me back the way we had come to the now silent jetty. The boat lay moored in the moonlight. We stepped into the boat and we headed back to the shore. As we got nearer, you could see the campfires still burning brightly. We arrived at the shore's edge. I stepped from the boat and immediately started to grow back to my normal size. Fairy

Nough turned the boat round and pushed it away from the shore. It turned and started to steer itself back to the island as if some invisible hand was guiding it.

'Come,' she said, 'back to bed. I will see you on the morrow.'

Soon I was snuggled next to the giant dogs and drifted off into a deep sleep.

13

Before I knew it the sun had started to come up over the horizon, a bright-red spot set in a bright-blue sky. Higher and higher it rose, pouring down its warm rays over our bodies. Oh how wonderful it felt – you could almost have forgotten the dangers that lay ahead.

The camp became a hive of activity, everyone doing their bit ready for the long march ahead. Mr Trinity strode over. Sutherland was still asleep and snoring his head off. I gave him a nudge in the back and he woke with a start. 'What . . . what . . . ?' he stammered as he rubbed his eyes.

'Good morning, Mr Trinity,' we both said.

'Good morning, boys! Let's sit by the fire, and have some breakfast. I have a treat for you.'

Sutherland and I got up and walked towards the fire. I could smell a wonderful aroma. We stopped in amazement. There in a large round frying pan were sausages, bacon and eggs!

'This is for you! . . . What do you call it? Full English breakfast? Enjoy it because after today it's back to *our* food, so tuck in!'

We sat down and filled our plates until they were over-flowing at the sides. I even took two large pieces of bread and made a large 'belly buster' sandwich. 'That's to keep for later,' I explained. Mr Trinity looked at me and smiled, shaking his head.

As we sat eating, a shout came from the edge of the shore; it was one of the Sondron men.

'Look, look!' he was shouting in an excited voice, We dropped our plates and ran towards the edge of the shore. Everyone was running around picking up their weapons, not knowing what to expect. We all stood at the shore. Fairy Nough hovered in front of Mr Trinity. 'Don't worry! It's my father.' We looked into the distance and I could just make out a small boat with a figure standing in the bow. Up above the sky was black, as if covered by some large rain cloud except that it was buzzing like a swarm of bees on the move.

As the boat neared the shore I could see King Ronough standing at the helm. He was dressed in a black skintight suit with a silver belt and shoes. On his head was a helmet with two gold wings either side. He had a crossbow slung across his right shoulder and a pouch of arrows over his left. The boat landed at the shore's edge and he stepped from it. He was quite tall, I noticed, for a fairy. He waved his hand and the black swarm descended onto the shore. To my surprise, I now saw that the 'bees' were hundreds of fairy warriors, each dressed in the same black suit and gold helmets with crossbows and arrows.

The King did not acknowledge me; clearly he did not want anybody to know that we had met the previous evening. He came towards Mr Trinity and bowed at the waist. He stood back up and said in a deep gravelled voice, 'So pleased to meet you, Mr Trinity. I see you have gathered a formidable army about you. We, too, have come to offer our services. For what you did for my daughter, Fairy Nough, I will forever be in your debt.'

'Thank you,' said Mr Trinity, bowing deeply. 'Come, let me introduce you to the other generals and friends that have gathered together in our struggle . . .'

King Ronough set off to the main campfire with Mr Trinity and the other leaders. We all sat down and Mr

Trinity took the Crystal Globe from his cloak and placed it on the ground in full view of everyone. He passed his hands over the whole Globe and rubbed it gently. The mist in the Globe started to clear.

'Look, King Ronough,' Mr Trinity said. 'Look, see what we are up against.'

And there in the Globe were the most horrible-looking creatures you could imagine, as if they had been put together like some Frankenstein monster. I had never seen such ugliness. There were giants with one eye and others with eyes protruding on stalks. There were creatures with three legs and others with huge humpbacks. There were thousands of misfits, grunting and waving weapons around their heads. grunting and shouting 'Zaker, Zaker, Zaker. It was terrifying, like a scene from Hell.

'Look, everybody, that's what we are up against,' said Mr Trinity.

We looked deeper into the Globe. The sky above was black with flying monsters, blocking out the sunlight.

'Silvienes!' Christinos said through clenched teeth.

A few of the hideous creatures had perched on a hillside, their bloodshot eyes darting to and fro and their beaks making a chattering noise. Sometimes they showed their razor-sharp teeth . . .

The mist started to appear in the Globe again and the terrible vision faded.

Everyone sat in silence.

General Dylantos spoke first: 'Well, quite a sight that was. We need more people. We're outnumbered by at least ten to one.'

'But we have more fighting skills on our side,' Mr Trinity said.

'Still not enough to defeat such a vast and deadly army,' argued Christinos.

King Ronough interrupted. 'Well, there is King Gandelin

and Queen Lindis of the Volsci. They have the largest army of anyone, even if it is for show. I have to admit, though, they are phenomenal warriors!'

Everyone shook their heads.

Enceladus spoke, keeping his booming voice as low as he possibly could for the sake of the fairy King. 'Yes, but their lands are to the west of us, at least three days' march away across the Ipichatau Mountains. It's a difficult terrain and extremely cold, and it might be a wasted journey even if we get there.'

Everyone sat in stony silence, staring into the now dying campfire.

Christinos spoke. 'We can't give up now. Too much is at stake. Do you want to become slaves to those creatures for the rest of your lives? Or, worse, their food supply! I don't. I haven't come this far to turn back now.'

King Ronough spoke up. 'I have a plan that will take at least two days off the journey. You don't *all* have to go. My daughter can go with some of my men and a dozen of General Giedroyc's Tyrocdiles for added protection. After all, they can fly; you can't. I think that solves the problem. My daughter is a very good friend of Queen Lindis, which might help us. Young John here is also a good friend to my daughter. He can go to help put our case forward to the King and Queen.'

'One snag,' Mr Trinity interrupted, 'young John can't fly! He's human.'

'Don't worry about a little thing like that,' King Ronough said. 'Just watch.' He took what looked like a small trumpet from his belt and began to blow. It let out a noise so shrill that we had to cover our ears with our hands. Out of the horizon came what looked like a white cloud, and as it got closer I realised it was a large seagull, all white with a dark circle around each eye and a bright yellow beak. It flew round a couple of times above our heads and then landed on the shore.

King Ronough arose from the campfire. 'Come, young sir, I want you to meet Portis. She is a friend of ours. We found her as a chick and was brought up as Fairy Nough's pet.'

Portis was about the size of a donkey. 'This is your transport to the land of the Volsci!' Mr Trinity laughed his approval.

We headed towards the bird, and, as we did so, the bird seemed to panic a little, its large brown eyes darting around in their sockets. Fairy Nough flew towards it and gently stroked its yellow beak. It instantly began to calm down.

'Come, John,' she said.

Cautiously I shuffled up to the bird, not knowing what to expect.

'Come, come, don't be afraid! She won't bite you,' Fairy Nough said in her high-pitched voice which was like a mouse squeaking.

I reached the head of the bird, its huge brown eyes now fixed on me.

'Hold out your hand,' Fairy Nough said. I held out my hand and in it she laid two small sugar lumps. 'Now put them up to her beak.' The bird opened its beak and ever so gently took them from the palm of my hand. She held her head back and swallowed. She then bent her head forward again and began to nestle against the small of my neck.

'John,' Fairy Nough said, 'I want you to meet Portis. Say hello to her!'

'Hello, Portis,' I said. She cooed back.

'Good, good,' Fairy Nough said. 'Now you are friends.'

King Ronough took Fairy Nough to one side and gave her instructions to give to King Gandelin. 'Guard them well.

These are the plans of how many soldiers we have, but you should be all right. Dr Zaker and his warriors are still too far north, But one can't be too careful. Take care and have a safe journey. Come, young John, climb on!'

The bird raised one leg and I stepped onto its bony kneecap, pulled myself up, and settled down into a small hollow just behind the bird's neck. Fairy Nough settled in front of me.

King Ronough bade us farewell. 'Take care of Fairy Nough for me – she's very precious.'

'Goodbye, Father,' Fairy Nough said. She patted Portis on the head and off we set along the sand and then high into the air. She circled round the camp a couple of times – everyone was waving – and then off we set into the sky.

We were followed by some of King Ronough's soldiers – I counted fifteen – and ten of General Giedroyc's men brought up the rear. As we flew higher I could see the Ipichatau Mountains in the distance, a mass of white snow-covered rocks, their peaks disappearing into the white and grey clouds above. On and on we went, the mountains getting nearer and bigger. We travelled for hours until Fairy Nough said, 'We will have to land soon. Portis will be getting tired. There's a small island up ahead – we'll rest there for the night.'

I looked up ahead and there it was, the island – it was unlike any other island I had ever seen. Normally you have the sea, then sand and finally trees and shrubs in the middle. This was different. You had the sea round the island then a large circle of trees and shrubs and a large sandy clearing in the middle. We landed in the clearing.

King Ronough's and General Giedroyc's soldiers also descended into the clearing. Fairy Nough and I climbed down off Portis and I began to gather wood from the surrounding forest to make a fire for the night. Everyone was busily going about their duties. Portis had settled down not far from the campfire that was starting to burst into life, The red and yellow flames quickly warmed the clearing and threw strange shadows all around us. All you could see of Portis was a large ball of feathers as she had tucked her head and legs tucked under her body. She looked like a round white boulder. Right in the middle of the clearing, I lay back and looked up at the stars that shone down through the trees. My bed was made of moss and leaves that I had gathered from the edge of the clearing. I sank deeper into the soft moss, making me feel warm and cosy. My eyes began to feel heavy with sleep and I soon drifted into a deep sleep.

14

I stirred the following morning as someone or something touched my face. I woke to find myself staring into the eyes of Portis. She was moving her beak up and down my cheek, her big eyes staring at me from under her long eyelashes. I held out my hand and began stroking her head, the soft feathers moving through my fingers.

Fairy Nough flew across to me and hovered next to my ear and quietly whispered, 'Come on, John, time to go!' I rose from my soft bed and brushed myself down, removing the moss and leaves from my clothes. King Ronough's soldiers along with General Giedroyc's men were dousing the fire and burying it in the sand. Fairy Nough said, 'It's best no one knows we've been here. Come, we should hurry. We have a half a day's flying before we reach the lands of the Volsci.'

I jumped upon Portis's back with Fairy Nough sitting in front of me like the day before. Portis trotted to one side of the clearing and began her take-off. Her wings flapped faster and faster as we rose into the air and it was not long before we were nearly to the other side of the clearing. I closed my eyes and thought, *Oh, no, we're going to hit the trees!* Suddenly, however, she whooshed straight up into the sky, missing the treetops by just a few inches. I gave a huge sigh of relief. Fairy Nough just smiled as if nothing was really the matter with the way Portis had flown us into air. She circled once round the island to get her bearings and then headed out across the Inland Sea towards the Mountains of Ipicha-tau and the land of the Volsci.

Ahead of us rose a mountain chain all covered in its coats of snow and ice. As we flew nearer, I could see what looked like some sort of protective wall, and a narrow pass filled with a thin white mist that led towards it. Out of the distance came a large bird-like creature – about the size of one of those dinosaur birds that I had seen in my school-books. Its bat-like wings spread either side of it, not flapping but gliding towards us. Its long beak and head moved gently from side to side as it flew. On its back was a man. He did not look a tall man and he was dressed in a black tunic, black helmet and had a pitch-black beard that highlighted his pale white face. Attached to the bird's neck on a kind of harness was a large crossbow and on either side of the crossbow were sheaths of bolts, about the size of whaling harpoons.

By this time King Ronough's men and the Tyrocdiles had formed a defensive shield around us, their weapons at the ready. Fairy Nough held up her tiny hand to everyone as if to say, 'Leave this to me.' The large bird had come alongside us and I looked across at the man on the creature. His jet-black eyes were staring at Fairy Nough and me, looking us up and down. Fairy Nough rose from her seat in front of me and began to fly across to the man on the other bird. She started to talk to him, her lips just moving, though no sound seemed to be coming from them. All I could hear was the flapping of Portis's wings and some strange gulping noise from her throat, which I guessed was fear. I didn't feel that confident myself either.

After about ten minutes Fairy Nough came back and settled into her seat.

'Are we going to be bird meat?' I gasped.

Fairy Nough just turned her head and smiled. She

reached down and stroked Portis's neck as if to reassure her. 'No, you'll be fine!'

The man on the large bird signalled for us to follow him. Off he went to the front of us and we followed behind. As we neared the entrance to the pass, we saw men patrolling up and down on the walls that protruded from either side of the mountains. On both walls were large crossbows, each one loaded and ready to fire at any intruder that came by either land or air. The men were dressed in the same black uniform and helmet as the man on the bird. Each one carried a bow and a sheath of arrows, and a short sword hung by his side. As we flew between the two parapets, I could see there were two doors on each side of the mountains with soldiers coming from them. They ran to their crossbows and took up their positions behind each one as if ready to fire upon us.

The Volsci warrior on the bird quickly took a small horn from a bag, put it to his lips and blew a deep sound, like a low rumble of thunder across the sky. The lookouts from either mountain blew their horns in reply and allowed us to pass freely into the narrow mountain pass. We followed the Volsci warrior along the pass through swirling mists, and then suddenly the mist cleared away. There below us was a valley full of green fields with a river running through it. The valley was surrounded by mountains on three sides and clinging to the mountainsides were numerous houses hollowed out of the solid rock. Each one had a small balcony, a large crossbow situated at the end, and gothic-style door with windows at either side. The houses were piled up one above the other just like a block of flats from my world. As we flew past, people rushed out onto the balconies to see us.

As we travelled along the valley floor, we saw people working in the fields tending the crops and also small boats with fishermen on the river. As we flew along, the valley began to get wider. The river now turned into a lake surrounded by green fields of corn and ahead of us was a mighty mountain. Protruding from its side was a breath-taking palace that could have been straight out of a picture book. It was dazzling white and its tall turrets, topped with gold and silver, glinted in the early-morning sunshine.

At the edge of the lake, on a small sandy beach, a Volsci soldier was waving his hand in an up-and-down motion, which we took as a sign to land. Portis circled a couple of times and then came down to land on the beach followed by King Ronough's and General Giedroyc's soldiers. With Fairy Nough, I dismounted from Portis, who instantly lay down on the warm sand and tucked her legs and head under her body. In a few moments she was asleep.

'Don't worry!' Fairy Nough said to me, 'She does it all the time. She's an old, tired bird!'

I just smiled and looked up at the palace that towered above me, its gold and silver turrets shining in the morning sunlight. A large wooden door began to open slowly and soldiers began to pour out of the entrance. There were at least twenty men all dressed in black from head to toe except for a few who wore individual red, blue or white plumes in their helmets. The soldier with the red plume started barking out orders and the soldiers with the white plumes formed a line either side of the door. The soldier with the blue plume stood to one side.

'Attention!' shouted the soldier with the red plume.

Everyone stood to attention, not moving a muscle, as if they were made from stone.

'Take over, Sergeant,' he shouted to the soldier with the blue plume.

'Yes, Sir,' he replied in a deep voice that sounded as if someone was scraping a stick along a wall.

The soldier with the red plume strode forward towards us. He was quite tall and lean with deep-set dark eyes and very bushy eyebrows. He had a small scar just under his left eye. Fixed to his chest were two small stars with a line through each one. From his right side hung a sword and from his left a small black dagger. He strode towards Fairy Nough, clicked his heels together, and made a slight bow. He then raised his head and spoke in a smooth quiet voice. 'Welcome to the land of the Volsci Princess. My name is General Rol and I wish to welcome you on behalf of Queen Lindis and King Gandelin.'

'Thank you, General.'

'Follow me!' the General said. We headed for the large wooden door and we all marched through in single file into a great hall. The Volsci soldiers followed us and the great big wooden door closed behind us with an almighty thud. General Rol turned to Fairy Nough. 'Your escort can bed down in that room over there, but you and your companion must follow me.'

Fairy Nough and I walked towards a door at the far end of the great hall, which was hung with shields and all types of armoury. We passed a long oak table – it must have been at least twenty feet long – and it was surrounded by heavy oak chairs whose backs were carved in the shape of a mighty bird, just like the one the guide had been mounted on.

We reached the door at the end of the great hall. General Rol knocked. 'Enter!' a voice boomed, the sound echoing around the hall. General Rol opened the door and Fairy Nough and I stepped through. There in front of us at the far end sat Queen Lindis and King Gandelin.

'Ah, Fairy Nough, so good to see you!' the King said. 'I heard about your troubles on your way here for my wedding a while ago. I'm so glad to see you are well and in good health.'

He and the Queen arose from their tall satin-backed chairs and came towards us. Their gold robes reached just over their jewelled shoes and brushed the ground as they walked. The Queen was tall and slim with long black hair that hung down to her waist. She was quite pale, with not much colour in her cheeks, but very beautiful. King Gandelin, on the other hand, was a large portly man, robust and round-featured with a small red beard and short-cropped hair. He had a jewelled headband on like Queen Lindis.

He strode forward to greet us. He bent down and took Fairy Nough's hand in his short stubby fingers and shook it gently.

'So glad to see you!' he said again. 'Come now, Fairy Nough, introduce me to your friend and tell us why you have brought some of your soldiers and General Giedroyc's men with you to our peaceful homeland.' His voice was soft, almost beseeching, which seemed quite strange in such a big man.

'It's a long story,' Fairy Nough said. 'And this is why I came with other soldiers – nothing is as it seems outside your world anymore.'

'Come, let's eat and you can tell me all about it,' replied the King.

Queen Lindis took my hand. 'And you are John?'

'Yes,' I said with a slight stammer.

'Come,' she said and led me to a staircase that was at the end of the room. We entered under a stone archway and began to climb up the narrow spiral staircase, one behind the other. We reached the top and King Gandelin opened a small door. He ushered us into a large square room with a marble fireplace at one end. Logs were blazing away in the fire warming the room. There were windows along one side and a door that led out onto a balcony. The other walls were decorated with portraits, which, as I later found out, were earlier kings and queens of the Volsci. There were two large sofas either side of the large fire. The room was dotted around with oak furniture and a large patterned rug lay on the floor. At one end of the room was an oblong dining table with eight chairs and on the table a big six-tiered candlestick. A chandelier hung from the ceiling. 'Sit by the fire,' King Gandelin said. 'We shall eat and then you can tell me your story.' He picked up a bell and gave it three sharp rings.

A door opened from the far side of the room and three servants came out. Each one carried a large oval dish covered with a silver cover, which was decorated with a bird's head finial. Another servant came out with large flagons of wine and water. They then all disappeared through the same door that they had come through.

As we ate Fairy Nough told the story of Mr Trinity's quest and how I came to be here. As she told him of the doings of Dr Zaker, King Gandelin grunted and nodded, but he really seemed to be more interested in the food. He took a napkin from the table and let out a great belch, then wiped his fingers and the juice from his beard.

'Ah, um,' he said, 'I think I will have to sleep on it and put it to the General in the morning. We'll see what he says. After all, this is a democratic nation, and I can't say anything without the General and his cabinet, though my say will go a long way.'

Queen Lindis took my arm. 'Rest now till morning.' She ushered me into a small bedroom at the other side of the room.

She closed the door behind me and I looked around. It had a big four-poster bed but it was otherwise sparsely furnished. It had a chair in one corner, a dressing table with a candlestick and a rug beside the bed. I removed my clothes, jumped in between the blankets on the bed, and lay my head on the soft pillows. I looked out of the small window at the side of the room at the stars and drifted off into a deep sleep.

*

I awoke to people talking in the other room. I crept to the door and slowly turned the handle. It opened slightly and I peered through the crack. I could see Fairy Nough sitting at the edge of the table alongside the King and Queen. Down the other side of the table sat General Rol and some more soldiers, all with red plumes in their helmets. I gathered these must be the generals. They were all talking among themselves.

I was watching through the gap in the door when Fairy Nough spotted me. She flew towards the open door and before I could close it, she was there, right in my face, hovering in front of me, her wings making a humming sound as they moved in the air. She waved her tiny finger at me and said in her soft voice that I could tell had a little bit of anger in it.

'It's bad manners to eavesdrop,' she said. 'Come, have some breakfast. It's time you were up anyway!' I walked towards the table. Everyone was beginning to leave except General Rol and the King and Queen. There was another man sitting with them dressed in the same black uniform with the same insignia as General Rol. His helmet was lying in front of him on the table, its red plume neatly brushed back. Like the King he was a portly man and his stomach bulged out over this red belt. He was clean shaven and had short-cropped blond hair. His eyes were a piercing blue that seemed to look right through you, sending shivers down your back. 'Ah, John,' King Gandelin said, 'Come and meet General Travin. He is the Commander of the Bird Squadron that guided you to us.'

General Travin stood up and I noticed he was short. 'Pleased to meet you,' he said in a sharp voice. He held out his hand towards me and I took his hand in mine – his grip was tight like a vice. He shook my hand vigorously, then let go and sat straight down in his chair again.

King Gandelin spoke: 'I have discussed the situation with

members of my government and the generals and we have agreed to give you some troops. I think, didn't you say, Travin, we can spare two thousand.'

I stepped back in amazement. Didn't he know that the future of his whole world was at stake if Dr Zaker and Kaunn won. He would not be king anymore; there wouldn't even be a kingdom!

I was about to say something when Fairy Nough looked at me, her eyes piercing into mine. She put her finger to her lips as if to say, 'Be quiet!' She came up close to me, and whispered in my ear. 'It's better than nothing. We will have to manage.'

'Come, I will show you what troops you can have. I'm sorry I can't give you more,' the King said, 'but I have to keep some back just in case . . . I think you know what I mean.'

Fairy Nough nodded. 'I understand,' she said. 'I want to thank you. It will be a great help.'

'Follow me,' the King said. He told the generals to get the men ready. They stood to attention, bowed and put on their helmets, then turned and walked smartly out of the room. In turn, we followed King Gandelin out of another door and up another staircase. I was getting quite out of breath as we climbed. We must have been climbing for about fifteen minutes when in front of us appeared yet another wooden door. King Gandelin opened it and a rush of wind nearly blew me off my feet. We stepped through the open door into bright sunlight. In front of me were mountains on three sides. I looked at King Gandelin.

'Yes, young man,' he said, 'we have walked to the other side of the mountain. Our home is actually the mountain.

'Come, onto the balcony.'

I stepped onto the balcony and gripped King Gandelin's arm. 'Follow me,' he said. I walked along the balcony to where a ledge was jutting out from the side of the mountain.

There was a small wall at the front of the ledge which offered protection from the wind that was blowing through my hair. I shuffled along close to the wall towards the ledge. I reached the edge of the balcony and looked at the ledge across from me. King Gandelin stepped onto the small ledge – it was just big enough to stand on with your back against the side of the mountain.

'You're quite safe,' he said. I stepped onto it followed by Fairy Nough. I started to breathe more slowly as the thought of falling began to ease. I took in my surroundings. Across from me was the most magnificent waterfall. As the water cascaded down, the wind blew spray away from the waterfall, and caught the light of the morning sun, making a dazzling display of rainbows. I had never seen anything so beautiful as what lay in front of me. The snow-covered mountains showed bits of of green where the early spring sun had begun to melt the snow. Even the snow glistened with colour as the sun shone on the droplets of water as it melted. Small ledges jutted out from the mountain and on these were about a hundred birds' nests. Sitting on each nest was one of the extraordinary Volsci steeds, squawking and flapping their great wings to and fro in the air.

I pulled King Gandelin's sleeve and asked what they were.

'That, young John, is what you might call our air force.' I smiled – at least there was one phrase we had in common, though he would have been amazed to see what passed for an air force in our world. I plucked up courage and leaned gingerly over the wall and looked down. Far below were soldiers running everywhere, busily going about their business.

'Come,' said King Gandelin to Fairy Nough and me, 'we will go down and watch the troops get ready for the journey.' We left the ledge and balcony and headed back down the stairs again, passing door after door that led into the different rooms of the palace. King Gandelin and Fairy Nough were talking as they descended. It was all right for her – she could just fly down! My legs ached as if I had run a marathon. Just when I thought that I would run out of breath we finally reached the bottom.

King Gandelin pushed open a large wooden door and we stepped into the sunlight. Generals Rol and Travin came running over. They stood to attention and saluted. 'Carry on,' the King said. They bowed slowly and then hurried away, shouting sharply at the soldiers.

On the ground, laid out in a single row, were forty large baskets, each fitted with four small wooden wheels, two front and two at the back. At the front of the basket was a large pole rising vertically up with a piece of wood across the top forming a letter T. There was a similar pole at the back of the basket. At the end of each piece of wood on the top were two hooks. The soldiers were running round gathering their weapons together – crossbows, swords and small daggers. Each soldier had at least twenty daggers around his waist and each dagger was at least six inches in length. As they ran towards the baskets each one picked up a round highly polished shield that gave off a dazzling silver glare. They reached the baskets and clamped their shields onto the sides.

I tugged on King Gandelin's robe. He turned and looked down at me.

'Yes, young John.'

'Excuse me, but what are those baskets for?' I asked.

'They will carry the troops on their journey – forty baskets with forty-eight troops in each. See the large birds – the Synisaurous . . . they are the pilots! There are eighty birds in all and that makes the two thousand troops.'

The troops began to climb into the baskets, while at the front and back a soldier stood on a small risen platform.

'Look!' said King Gandelin, 'Look up there!' I looked

up to where the birds were. Now on each of the bird's back sat a soldier, just behind the large crossbow attached to it. Each bird let out a screaming squawk, then spread their wings and began to drop from the ledge. They opened up their wings and took one large flap and they were in the air. One by one, they circled above the baskets full of soldiers. Now I noticed that each bird had a round hook dangling from each leg. Down they came one by one, flew towards the baskets and gripped the wooden poles. The soldiers, meanwhile, hooked a chain onto the outstretched legs of the birds, and the baskets started to roll along the floor, their wheels rumbling over the sandy floor.

All of a sudden, they were in the air! It was a fantastic sight as they started to disappear into the clouds above them. Suddenly they were gone and there was nothing but silence.

'Come, we have to leave now. After all, we don't want to be last for the fight, do we?' King Gandelin said.

We headed back the way we came, back to the clearing where Portis was. There in front of me was the biggest bird I had ever seen, much bigger than all the other ones. On its back was a small basket that held about six people. I asked King Gandelin what creature that was. 'That,' he said proudly, 'is *my* transport!' She is a Migasaurous and one of a kind. Isn't she magnificent? We will travel by her. My bird creatures don't have to stop, unlike Portis.'

I looked around for King Ronough's troops and the Tyrocdile soldiers. Fairy Nough spoke to me. 'Don't worry, they left last night. They have to stop on the way; we don't!'

Queen Lindis came out carrying what looked like chain-mail, a large sword and a crossbow. Behind her a servant girl carried a helmet, with a bright-yellow plume.

'Here, my King,' she said. 'May the Gods be with you and bring you victory and a trouble-free return!'

King Gandelin and I ran to the Migasaurous. A soldier

threw down a rope and King Gandelin clambered into the basket. He reached down, took my arm, and pulled me in after him. Fairy Nough was already seated in a small chair at the back of the basket.

The King busied himself putting on his chainmail armour.

'Sit down, young man,' he said in an excitable voice. 'Oh what an adventure!' He turned round, and now all you could see was his red beard sticking out from his helmet and his eyes peeking through. He took off his helmet and placed it on the basket floor. He sat down on a chair next to Fairy Nough and I sat on another chair at the side. 'Is everyone ready?' the King asked.

'Yes,' we replied in unison. 'Pilot,' he shouted to the soldier at the front, 'Let's fly!'

15

The soldier pulled on the reins attached to either side of the bird's beak by a small hook fixed to a round ring in its beak. The bird started to run along the ground, its great wings flapping and making a noise like thunder. I hung onto the side of the basket as it began to move. Suddenly we were in the air. We flew along the valley floor and past the houses on the mountain. Everyone was waving and I watched as the people grew smaller and smaller as we began to climb higher and higher.

Eventually we were enveloped by damp white clouds, but only for a couple of minutes and then we emerged into bright sunlight and clear blue skies. It felt quite warm and my clothes that had been dampened by the clouds began to dry.

'Look, look!' King Gandelin shouted, 'There, ahead of us!'

I looked into the distance and all I could see was a dark formation in front of me. It got bigger and bigger. It was Generals Rol and Travin with the rest of the troops. Nearer and nearer we got, the large Migasaurous gliding effortlessly along. We passed alongside and took the lead. I looked back and every Synisaurous had made an arrow formation behind us. On we flew, picking up speed, until we turned east into the sun and headed for the beach where everyone was waiting for our arrival.

I looked back at the mountains with their snow-topped peaks, watching them grow smaller and smaller until they were out of sight. There was nothing below us but the blue sea – the clouds had disappeared – and there was nothing but blue sky. As I looked down, I could see the shadows of the birds and the baskets on the water.

'We should be there by nightfall,' King Gandelin said.

I looked at him with astonishment. After all, it had taken us two days to get to his land.

'I know what you are thinking, young John – why so quick? Well, young man, these large creatures travel at least twice the speed of Portis and General Giedroyc's men and King Ronough's soldiers. Look ahead, young man, there's the island you rested on the first night.'

I looked down at the island as we flew over, at the dark green trees with the soft white sand in the centre.

'Sit back and enjoy the journey,' the King advised. I sat back in my small seat and let the warmth of the sun soak into my body. Soon I drifted off to sleep to the rhythmic sound of the Migasaurous's wings beating up and down. It seemed only a moment later that Fairy Nough woke me, pulling on my ear and whispering, 'Time to wake up now. We're nearly there.'

I rubbed my eyes and looked around me. The sun was just starting to lower onto the horizon, turning the sea and sky a fiery red as if they had caught fire.

'Look, look!' Fairy Nough said. In the distance were the campfires of the soldiers, dotted about all over the place, hundreds of them, each one throwing out a yellow flame. We got nearer and lower. I could see everyone running about excitedly, and some of the Sondron men were beginning to light fires on either side of a field, making a landing strip. By now the sun had disappeared below the horizon and only the moon and the fires illuminated the night sky. King

Gandelin gave orders to land. 'Yes, my King,' the pilot shouted.

The great Migasaurous circled the landing strip once and then started to come down, its great wings flapping as we came in to land between the landing strip fires, its long legs pounding along the ground. Finally it spread its wings in a horizontal motion to act like some sort of brake and we came to a halt at the end of the field. At once the great bird dropped onto its large belly.

King Gandelin, Fairy Nough and I leapt from the basket and ran away from the landing strip, as other birds were now coming in to land. The great bird, too, rose up and with a huge bound, ran to the far end of the field out of the way. King Gandelin picked up a burning stick and waved it above his head in a back-and-forward motion. I looked up and all I could see were the shadows of the Synisaurouses as they circled under the moonlight. It was a beautiful, eerie sight.

The night air was filled with the sound of the great birds as they descended. The baskets touched down and the wheels rattled over the hard ground. The soldiers at the front and back of each basket shouted to each other in unison and reached up and unhooked the basket from the Synisaurouses' great legs. The birds picked up speed again and rose into the night sky squawking as they went before disappearing into the darkness. As the baskets came to a halt, the soldiers jumped out and began to push their vehicle to one side, out of the way of the other incoming birds and baskets. One by one they landed, forty baskets, one after the other.

When every one had landed safely, King Gandelin waved the burning stick in a circular motion above his head and one by one the Synisaurouses circled once and began to come down again to land in a nearby field, and settle down for the night. Some of the Volsci soldiers busied themselves with feeding the birds, throwing them huge chunks of meat that the creatures swiftly devoured making horrible squawking noises as they did so. As the birds ate, the pilots hammered long metal spikes into the ground and attached each of the birds to them using long chains. Finally King Gandelin's soldiers stood in single file to attention at the end of the runway.

I turned and saw coming towards me Sutherland, Mr Trinity, the two Poppies, Christinos, Judithos, Enceladus and Alcyoneus, with King Ronough and General Dylantos at the rear. As they approached, Mr Trinity held out his hand to King Gandelin, who took it in his and shook it vigorously.

'Welcome,' Mr Trinity said. 'Thank you for coming! We are ever so grateful.'

'You must be Mr Trinity,' the King said. 'I've heard so much about you. It's an honour for me to be here.'

'Thank you,' Mr Trinity said. 'Come, let me introduce you to everyone. You must be hungry.'

'Thank *you*,' the King replied. 'And let me introduce you to Generals Rol and Travin . . .'

After everyone had introduced themselves, King Gandelin told his generals to settle the men down for the night. Mr Trinity invited the King and the generals to join him for a meal by the campfire. Everyone headed for the large campfire where what looked like a deer was roasting over a spit above the roaring fire. On the way Mr Trinity put his hand on my shoulders. 'You must tell us about your journey, John.'

And so, when we all settled comfortably by the fire and happily tucking into the roast meat, I started to tell everyone about the journey and the fantastic sights I had seen in the land of the Volsci and what it was like to fly with those great birds. I talked and talked until my jaws began to ache.

Eventually Mr Trinity interrupted me with the wave of his hand. 'Some adventure!' he said with a wry smile. He knew that I had put things in to make it more exciting than it really was. After all, nothing got past him and his uncanny ability to read other people's thoughts. 'Now, young man, off to bed with you! It will be a busy day tomorrow.'

Sutherland and I picked ourselves up and went to lie down beside the giant dogs, cuddling into their long shaggy fur.

I awoke the next morning to the sound of hustle and bustle around the campfires. The soldiers were dousing the embers and gathering their weapons. Some were cleaning their swords and daggers; others were sharpening theirs on whetstones they had taken from the riverbed. I nudged Sutherland out of his noisy sleep; he had a funny habit of making a noise like a squeaky mouse. He sat up and rubbed his eyes.

'What . . . what?' he said.

'Come on!' I replied. 'Everyone's getting ready to move. We don't want to miss breakfast!'

He jumped up. 'No chance!'

I leapt to my feet and we both ran to the main campfire where Mr Trinity was sitting with the two Poppies. 'Boys,' Mr Trinity said, his eyes twinkling, 'just in time for breakfast!'

I looked down and there in the pan were some thick sizzling sausages and in another pan of boiling water two huge eggs, each the size of a football! 'Compliments of King Gandelin,' Mr Trinity explained. 'Birds' eggs . . . Please help yourselves.'

As we tucked in greedily, the other leaders joined us round the fire.

'Now down to business,' Mr Trinity said. With those words, he took the Crystal Globe from his cloak, placed it

117

down in front of him, and began to rub its smooth crystalline surface. It started to glow and a murky mist started to appear. The mist cleared and before us once again was Dr Zaker with Kaunn in all their finery looking down from a small hillock at the hideous troops below.

'Look,' I pointed, 'there's those bird-type creatures that attacked us in the forest and nearly killed Sutherland.'

'Ah,' said King Gandelin, 'I know what that is! It's an Angasaurous. They live far to the north in the lands of ice and snow. They will fight for anyone if the price is right. Scavengers, that's all they are,' he said in a disgusted voice. He spat on the ground. 'Don't worry, I've had dealings with those creatures before. My Synisarouses will take care of them . . .' I looked into the Globe and the whole sky seemed suddenly to be filled with these terrifying creatures, their half-human, half-bird heads moving from side to side as they looked around them.

'Dr Zaker's army just gets bigger and bigger,' Christinos said. 'Look, there are the Geynie.' She clenched both of her tiny hands, making her knuckles white. Everyone looked closer and there they were, those wolf-like creatures, their fangs dripping saliva as they savaged some poor creature, tearing bits of flesh off it and throwing their heads back and chewing on the flesh. Their fangs were blood-red, the same colour as their bloodshot eyes as they tore into the flesh repeatedly. Mr Trinity quickly picked up the crystal and put it back beneath his cloak.

Everyone sat there in stunned silence. Suddenly Alcyoneus brought his huge fist down, making the ground shake around us and sending sparks from the fire high into the blue sky. His face brimmed with anger, his eyes wide and wild. It sent shivers down my spine – I had never seen him like that before.

'We have to go on! We can't let them win! It will be the end of our lands if we do. Everywhere will be plunged into eternal darkness,' he bellowed. 'How many troops can we muster?' he asked Mr Trinity.

Mr Trinity looked around the leaders who answered one by one. 'Two thousand,' replied King Gandelin. 'One thousand,' said Christinos quietly. 'Same here!' shouted King Ronough. General Dylantos spoke: 'I have two thousand.'

'We also have General Giedroyc's Tyrocdiles,' said Mr Trinity. 'He will meet us at the next camp so I don't know how many he will bring. Master Remlin is visiting other lands, too, far to the north, the lands of the Ice People. I don't know how many men he can muster . . . with Alcyoneus's giants that makes six thousand . . .' Mr Trinity sighed. 'But we will win because good is on our side and that's why we will win this fight.'

We all sat for a moment in silence. Mr Trinity raised his hand and Honitos came shuffling along on his scrawny legs. His body bent forward, hands clasped together. 'Yes, Mr Trinity?'

'Bring us some of that wine you have and some beakers, please.'

Honitos bowed and shuffled away, and soon returned with the wine and beakers. Mr Trinity began to pour some into each beaker and handed them round to everybody round the fire.

'To victory!' Mr Trinity said.

'To victory!' everyone replied, then threw their wooden beakers onto the fire.

'Come, let's go,' Mr Trinity said.

Everyone rose and set off to their individual troops, while Sutherland and I doused the fire.

'Come,' said Mr Trinity, 'You two will travel with me. After all, how would I explain to Mrs Pickergill if anything happened to you two . . . My life wouldn't be worth living!' he added with a laugh.

16

I was riding behind Poppy Two. The sun was high in the sky and the sweat was running down my back and soaking the band round my trousers, making me feel rather uncomfortable. We had been marching for what seemed like hours. I looked up into the sunlight, shielding my eyes with the palm of my hand. I could see the Tyrocdiles moving slowly high above my head. The sunlight was reflecting off their silver uniforms making bright slivers of light that gave the sky an eerie glow.

We travelled on hour after hour. *Oh for a little rain to cool me down*, I thought to myself. The heat was unbearable. I looked across at Sutherland and he was hugging Poppy One close, trying to get some shade from Poppy's huge bulk. I looked around me at the other warriors. They all seemed to be suffering like Sutherland and me. Perspiration was running down their foreheads and making small droplets on their noses that then dripped off.

On and on we marched. I prayed for rain, I could not stop thinking of water. I was scanning the ground trying to take my mind off the heat, when a dark spot appeared in the dust. Then another and another. I looked up into the sky and felt a drop of water fall on my brow. It was rain! It started to come down more heavily and the ground turned dark brown. I held my head back to catch the drops in my mouth. They felt warm and tasted good. Now the rain was so heavy it bounced off the ground and big puddles appeared. Now a muddy plain lay before us, nothing around us but flat wet earth.

Mr Trinity galloped alongside. His hair was soaking wet, making it stick to his face. The rain was running off the end of his long thin nose. 'Don't worry, boys,' he said, 'it will soon stop. Apparently, General Dylantos says it rains this time every day.'

And, as if magic, the rain suddenly stopped and the sun started to dry the ground, creating a fine hazy mist. Soon, however, the sun started to settle on the horizon like a huge red fireball, making the sky bright red as if the whole of the world was on fire. In the distance I could make out several white lights and behind them a row of dark hills that lifted up from the dusty plain. Somehow the hills looked ominous.

We soon reached the campfires, which had been set up by Honitos and the Sondron men. By now it was completely dark except for the glow from the fires, which had been set out in a large circle. I could smell the food as it roasted over the open fires. We headed for the centre of the circle to a large fire in the middle of the camp. By the firelight I noticed the hills before me rising almost vertically into the night sky. They looked like sheer smooth rock from base to top except for a deep, black opening that seemed to lead into the hills. I shivered involuntarily. Suddenly I saw two red bloodshot eyes staring out of the opening. I nudged Mr Trinity and pointed.

'Don't worry! They can't attack. There are too many of us.' I felt quite uncomfortable, but I knew I was safe with all these soldiers.

After we had eaten Mr Trinity addressed the leaders: 'It won't belong now before it's time to meet Dr Zaker and Kaunn on the other side of those hills. It's maybe another day's march, so tonight we will have to think carefully about our strategy.'

121

Alcyoneus spoke. 'I will take some of my men on ahead first. After all we are the biggest, and we will have a better chance.'

Mr Trinity nodded his head and all agreed. Everyone was talking and eating and trying to make plans – what battle formations to use and what tactics. They were drawing different formations on the ground with small pointed sticks when King Ronough spoke up.

'We should guard that pass tonight. I'll put the two dogs at the entrance a few yards from the opening.'

General Dylantos agreed. 'I know that pass. It's long and narrow for about two miles and then it opens up onto a large flat plain. There are a few boulders scattered about which have fallen from the hillsides, and the grass is ten feet tall – perfect, in short, for an ambush. Beyond that is a vast desert – no trees, or cover of any description. In the distance beyond you can see the mountains of the Ice People where Master Remlin has gone.'

'Well, we'll just have to keep our eyes peeled when we go through,' said Mr Trinity.

Later that night, after everyone except the guards had gone to sleep, I was woken by the giant dogs' snarling. I nudged Sutherland, trying to wake him. He grunted in his usual whining way. When he finally woke from his sleep, Poppy One clasped a hand over his mouth.

'Be quiet,' he said in a whisper.

Mr Trinity, Enceladus, Alcyoneus and Poppy Two were sitting beside the fire. Enceladus and Alcyoneus were sharpening their long swords. At their sides on the ground were two large clubs with round heads studded with long steel spikes.

I sat down beside Mr Trinity. He put his finger to his lips, then pointed to the entrance of the pass. I gasped in horror. All I could see were dozens of bloodshot red eyes staring out at us from the blackness.

General Dylantos came and sat down next to Mr Trinity. 'My warriors are in place either side of the pass. Whatever comes out we will attack them from the rear. Judithos and Christinos will come in from the flanks. General Giedroyc's men will patrol the skies just in case something comes over those hills and Enceladus and the giants will form a circle round you just in case whatever is hiding in that pass is not friendly. After all, you'll be the one they're after.'

Mr Trinity nodded. Deep down I knew that, even now, Mr Trinity was not afraid. 'Just carry on as if nothing's the matter,' he said.

Alcyoneus whistled and the two giant dogs came bounding towards us and lay down in front of Mr Trinity. 'Extra protection!' he said.

We all sat round the fire talking and pretending as if we did not know what was going on. Poppy One and Two were telling jokes and everyone was laughing to keep up the pretence.

By now the fire in front of the pass had started to go out – there were just a few red and yellow embers flickering in the darkness. Suddenly loud piercing screams came from the pass, forcing you to cover your ears to shut out the noise. 'Everyone ready?' cried Mr Trinity. Everyone nodded.

Sutherland and I lay down close to the ground, and Mr Trinity took off his cloak and threw it over us.

'Don't move!' he said. 'And blacken your faces!'

We scraped some ash from the edge of the fire and used it to camouflage our faces. All I could see of Sutherland was two white eyes.

The screams got louder and louder, filling the night air and echoing around into the distance. Then they came, bounding out of the pass one by one.

'Geynie!' Alcyoneus shouted.

They ran towards us, saliva dripping from their giant fangs, their eyes bloodshot and wild. You could see every muscle and sinew in their bodies as they ran. You could see their veins as the blood ran through them. They kept on coming, one after the other, too many to count. They had a sword and short dagger in each claw-like hand and they screamed as they came hurtling towards us.

Alcyoneus and some of the Scordisi soldiers rushed out to meet them, a sword and a huge spiked club in each of their enormous hands. General Dylantos's men, meanwhile, closed in from the rear and shut off the pass. They were chopping and thrusting with their swords and with every blow you could hear the screams of these creatures as their swords cut into the thin bony flesh.

The Geynie corpses began to pile up around the perimeter of our campfire, their bodies crushed and broken into piles of scrawny bone and flesh. Blood was oozing everywhere and soaking into the ground, turning it into dark-red mud. I lay under Mr Trinity's cloak, my heart pounding like a drum. And all the time Mr Trinity just sat there, not moving a muscle, calmly watching the carnage that was going on all around us.

The fight raged on for at least two hours. As it neared its end, the sun was just starting to come over the horizon. There were Geynie bodies lying everywhere. Some had crushed heads, others broken bodies. Alcyoneus came towards Mr Trinity, his upper body covered in blood His huge frame was panting for breath.

'It's good exercise, Mr Trinity!' he said.

Mr Trinity smiled. 'Come out, boys! It's all over now.'

Sutherland and I crawled from under the cloaks and stood up. Poppy One and Two laughed at our blacked-out faces. They each threw us a pouch of water made from the skin of some animal.

'Wash your faces!' they said.

We watched as General Dylantos went across to one of the bodies and reach down. He snapped one of the fangs out of the lifeless head. 'Um,' he murmured, 'this will make a nice necklace!'

17

A little later as we sat over a meagre, but welcome, breakfast, we noticed the sky in the distance beginning to darken. It was like a big black cloud except this cloud was making a noise like a thousand birds. It sounded like wings flapping all at once in rhythm. Nearer and nearer, louder and louder the noise got. When the noise was above our heads it started to break up and come down onto the plain all around us. Finally it was General Giedroyc and his troops!

All the Tyrocdiles landed and General Giedroyc strode forward, his silver suit shining bright in the morning sunlight.

'Good morning, Mr Trinity. I see you've had a busy night!'

'So we have,' said Mr Trinity. 'But it's all over now. Come and sit by the fire and tell me about your journey.'

General Giedroyc headed to the campfire where Mr Trinity introduced him to everybody.

'Why the dark cloud formation, General?' asked King Ronough.

'Camouflage!' he replied. 'To fool people! It's basically an attack formation for us to get close to our enemies.'

'Very effective,' King Ronough said. 'We thought you were a flock of birds.'

'Thank you,' General Giedroyc said.

'Now down to business,' Mr Trinity said. 'We have to get

through that pass to the other side of those hills. We can't go round because it would take too long. Once we get through we'll be in Dr Zaker's territory then . . .'

'I think we should stay here another night,' General Giedroyc said. 'I will take some of my men and go over the hills tonight and get the lay of the land.'

Everyone nodded in agreement. 'That's a good idea,' said General Dylantos. 'It might give us an advantage when it comes to the time to fight.'

'We can't leave yet anyway,' said Christinos. 'My Sondron men are still out searching for food for the last leg of our journey.'

'Well, that's settled,' said Mr Trinity. 'We'll wait for dusk and General Giedroyc to bring us back some more information.'

All the leaders agreed and headed off to their respective parts of the camp to prepare for the march through the pass in the morning.

Sutherland and I lay down on the hard stony ground and let the sun beat down on our weather-beaten faces. We dozed in and out of sleep. We hadn't had have much rest the night before and it wasn't long before I dozed.

The next thing I knew was someone kicking the soles of my feet. It was Poppy One again.

'Come on, boys. It's teatime!'

My body ached from lying on the hard ground, but the thought of food made me quickly forget my discomfort. I could smell the food cooking over the open fire, the fat dripping onto the red embers making them sizzle with each droplet. Everyone was sitting round the fire tearing bits of meat from the carcass and licking the juices from around their lips.

King Gandelin started to speak, the meat juices still soaking his red beard.

'It will soon be dark. General Giedroyc will be leaving as soon as the sun sets.'

Already the darkness had begun to creep across the land and a full moon appeared from behind the passing clouds, casting deep shadows on the ground from the sides of the steep hills that lay in front of us.

'Time to go!' said General Giedroyc. 'I will take twenty men with me. We'll probably be away about two hours.' He strode off towards his men at the far side of the camp.

'Come,' said Mr Trinity, 'we'll see them off.' From a distance we watched the General's scouts fly up into the air. Soon all you could see was a dark shadow moving along in the moonlight like a dark rain cloud. Finally, they disappeared over the hilltops. We headed back towards the fire to keep warm while we waited. There was almost complete silence, except for the odd grunt from King Gandelin as he continued to tuck into the roast meal. We waited and waited. One hour turned into two and two into three. The sun was beginning to rise up over the horizon like a bright yellow fireball, the darkness fading away.

Suddenly General Dylantos shouted, 'Look!'

Everyone looked up at the sky. It was General Giedroyc and his men. I watched as they circled around us for a while, their silver suits shining in the morning sun.

They landed not too far away from the now dying campfire. General Giedroyc strode across towards Mr Trinity, looking extremely tired from his night-time reconnaissance. He sat down to the left of Mr Trinity and Poppy One handed him a flagon of water. The General drank greedily, most of it running down the side of his lips, soaking his silver uniform. After he had drunk his fill, he put down the flagon, took up a burnt stick from the fire, and began to draw a map into the hard soil.

'The hills in front of us are flat,' he explained. 'No bumps or mounds . . . just flat . . . They stretch for about five miles and then it's a steep drop straight down to grassland. *That* stretches for a further two miles. The grass is very long and ideal for an ambush. Once you get through the long grass there's a flat desert for as far as the eye can see . . .'

'Well, that confirms what we knew . . . At least, now we have a very accurate map of what we can expect,' said Mr Trinity.

'I'm sorry we're a bit late,' the General went on, 'We encountered some of those half-man, half-bird creatures . . .'

'Angasaurous, they're called,' interrupted Alcyoneus.

'Ah,' said General Giedroyc, 'Well, now there's ten less of them! Each one with a dozen arrows in its fat ugly body.'

King Gandelin spoke up: 'We can fly over the grassland. If there's anyone waiting in that long grass we will burn them out . . . We could even carry everyone over in the baskets . . . It would only take two or three trips. The only drawback is the giants. They're too big for the baskets! Plus we'll have to leave behind the food wagons. Everyone can carry extra food with them instead.'

General Dylantos disagreed. 'I really feel we need as much food as possible. We don't know how long that desert goes on for,' he said. 'I think we'll need to find a way of getting the wagons over those hills . . .'

The discussions went on for most of the morning. Everyone had their ideas, some more practical than others. As I listened I grew very drowsy. Surely we just needed to act quickly! Mr Trinity must have read my thoughts, for, glancing at me, he said with a smile, 'John's right. I think we have discussed enough. It's time to act.'

It was decided we would begin our journey across the hills that night, under cover of darkness. The sky was full of stars and everything seemed so peaceful – you would never have thought that we were trying to save the world of Sofala from the evil clutches of Dr Zaker and Kaunn. For some time now King Gandelin's birds had been taking off with their heavy loads of baskets, filled with men and provisions. All you could see were the shadows of the great birds moving over the ground, getting smaller and smaller as they flew out of sight. One by one they went until they were all gone, leaving the rest of us staring into the night sky.

'Now for the wagons!' cried King Gandelin. He was clearly relieved that we had decided to take those too. The giant Migasaurous swooped down and grasped one of the wagons in its huge claws and lifted it off the ground with ease.

King Gandelin said, 'One successful lift! Let's hope we can do more.'

An hour later and there was only Alcyoneus, Enceladus and Christinos left, along with Mr Trinity, King Gandelin, Sutherland, the two Poppies and me, and two hundred Sondron soldiers and three hundred of the giants. Fairy Nough had gone ahead with her father and his soldiers. The Migasaurous flew down ready for its final flight. Mr Trinity turned to Christinos. 'Will you be all right?' he said as he took her hand. He had a soft spot, I think, for her – after all, she was very beautiful.

'I'll be fine, don't worry!' she replied.

Mr Trinity smiled and nodded. 'I know,' he said, 'I know.'

King Gandelin interrupted. 'We have to go. It will be light in an hour.'

Mr Trinity, the two Poppies, Sutherland and I, along with the portly King Gandelin, headed for the Migasaurous and squeezed into the large basket on its back. The King signalled to the pilot and the great bird began to run along the hard flat ground, its beating wings making a thunderous noise as they flapped up and down in the air. All of a sudden we left the ground and circled once. Mr Trinity looked over the side and waved to Christinos below. She waved back, already a tiny figure far below.

We circled once more and headed for the hills in front of us. I looked down and could just see Christinos mounting her horse and the giant soldiers heading for the pass with Alcyoneus at the head . . . and then they were gone. Nothing below us now but the flat tops of the hills. I just hoped there was nothing waiting in that pass for them.

We flew over the hills and then grasslands, the great bird gliding gently so as not to make any noise. We landed on the edge of the desert plain just as the daylight began to come up over the horizon. It was very cloudy. There was no sun. It was going to be a dark day and rain clouds were already gathering in the distance. We dismounted from the Migasaurous and headed for King Ronough who stood debating with the generals.

'We have to burn that long grass,' he was saying. 'Big as the giants are, even they wouldn't stand much of a chance if they were ambushed. They would be butchered. We cannot take that chance. We have to burn the grass to make sure . . .' The fairy King's words were respected.

'He is right, Mr Trinity,' said King Gandelin. 'It has to be done. There is no choice. And we have to do it now. The rain clouds are gathering and, if it rains, that's it!'

Mr Trinity nodded. 'But can we burn it before Christinos and the Giants get to the end of the pass?'

General Giedroyc interrupted. 'I'll send two of my men into the pass to tell them to hold back until we have burnt it. If there *is* anyone in that grass, there's only one way out and that's back through the pass where Alcyoneus and Enceladeous will be waiting for them!'

Everyone nodded in agreement. General Giedroyc summoned two of his men and told them the plan. They saluted and took to the skies.

131

General Dylantos, meanwhile, summoned two dozen men, gave each one a burning torch, and told them to spread out fifty yards apart. They ran to the edge of the grass and waited for the signal. Everyone stood there in anticipation of the blaze and no small degree of apprehension in case anyone or anything should come running out of that long grass. Dylantos's soldiers lowered their burning torches into the grass and it instantly burst into flames, making a wall of yellow fire reaching upwards of twenty feet. Suddenly screams came from the long burning grass. The generals summoned their archers, who ran to the edge of the smouldering earth, got down on their knees, and readied their bows and crossbows. The screams grew louder as the flames began to move ever nearer to the base of the hills. Horrible-looking creatures began to pour out of the flames one after the other, their bodies on fire, waving their long arms and claw-like hands. The screams ran through you, making you cover your ears to shut out the unearthly noise.

General Dylantos gave the signal to fire and the archers let loose a volley of arrows. You could hear the sickening thuds as the missiles pierced the burning bodies. Arrow after arrow began to pour into them making them scream even louder. It wasn't a very pretty sight and the stench of burning flesh made your stomach churn.

By now the flames had reached the base of the hills. Burnt smouldering bodies lay all around on the scorched smouldering earth. The entrance to the pass was blocked off by blackened bodies where the creatures had tried to escape the inferno.

Only now did we turn away from the carnage and head for the circle of wagons that had been laid out in front of us, each one next to the other, wheel to wheel, with just one small entrance between two of them. We entered through the opening to find a small fire that Honitos and the Sondron men had made from a wagon that had broken up on landing the night before. They started to bring food from the wagon and set about preparing a meal. To be honest, for once I didn't feel hungry – not after what I had seen.

Sutherland and I sat down beside the small fire. At least the rain clouds had kept away. The day was bright now, the sun high in the sky, warming my aching bones. Mr Trinity walked towards us and sat down beside us at the fire.

'Sorry, boys,' he said. 'Not a very nice thing to see but those creatures would have killed you without a moment's hesitation. You have to understand that it's them or us. Just try to put it to the back of your mind.' He put his arm around my shoulder. I'd never felt so close to tears. I wanted, for the first time, to go home.

'I know,' Mr Trinity said. 'Christinos and Alcyoneus will be coming through the pass soon, I think we should go and meet them.' We both nodded, though I really didn't fancy walking over that scorched earth past burnt bodies. All the same I had to face my fears.

'Good,' said Mr Trinity. 'Come on then!'

As Sutherland and I walked with Mr Trinity, a lump came into my throat and panic started to set in. I looked across at Sutherland who was walking the other side of Mr Trinity. I could see the fear on his face and I suspected he could see mine, too. I started to slow as we got nearer to the edge of the blackened smouldering earth. I wanted to run but Mr Trinity gripped my left arm with his bony fingers, digging them into my flesh. 'You'll be fine,' he said reassuringly.

On we walked until finally we reached the edge of what had once been long green grass swaying in the wind. We began to pick our way through the smouldering bodies. Some were burnt to the bone with only bits of flesh hanging on here and there. On some you could just make out their evil faces now even more deformed by the ravages of the fire. I began to retch.

'Are you all right, young John?' Mr Trinity asked.

'I'm OK!' I replied quietly. I wiped my mouth and eyes on my sleeve, and we continued on our way across to the entrance of the pass. There we saw the pile of hideous corpses. It was a terrible sight, straight out of a nightmare. I wanted to scream. We stopped and stared. We couldn't take our eyes off these charred bodies.

Suddenly they began to move. I stepped back gripping Mr Trinity's cloak. Surely they weren't still alive?

The hideous pile fell to one side and there in front of me stood Alcyoneus with a broad smile on his face. He strode forward, followed by Enceladus and the other giants, and then out came Christinos. I looked at Mr Trinity whose expression now transformed into a big beaming smile. He could not stop himself from running up to her, but then he came over all shy. 'I'm so glad you're alright,' he said, but added, 'We could never do without such a valuable leader!'

Sutherland and I had to stop ourselves from laughing.

'Did you get through the pass without any trouble?' he asked her.

'Yes,' she replied, a smile coming to her face. 'I see you've been busy here!' she said.

Mr Trinity beamed again. 'And that's just the beginning of your revenge.'

We walked back towards the camp and reached the campfire where King Gandelin sat with the other generals tucking into a meal. It was just another day's work to them.

18

The day had been a long one and the sun started to sink down over the horizon leaving a clear moonlit sky dotted with stars. I lay back and looked up at the night sky, thinking of home. Would I ever get back or was this some sort of dream I was living in? With my thoughts spinning around in my head, I fell into a deep sleep.

I awoke to someone gently kicking my ankle. I slowly opened my eyes and looked up. It was Poppy One grinning through his large black beard.

'Did you enjoy your sleep, young John?' he said. 'It's time to get up. Wake Sutherland and then both of you come over to breakfast. We've another long day in front of us.'

I kicked Sutherland and he awoke muttering to himself as he always did.

'Come on,' I said, 'we're wanted. It's breakfast.'

I got up and put on my shoes, which by now looked very tatty. We went to the campfire and sat down next to Poppy One and Two, who handed us great big plates of food. After everyone had eaten their fill, Mr Trinity began to speak.

'We will have to be careful now. We're getting near to Dr Zaker. I don't think he'll risk attacking in the desert; he'll wait until we come to him. He will count on us being tired from the long marches we've done these past few days. I know how he thinks ... How many troops have we got now?' he asked the other generals.

'Seven thousand altogether,' came the reply.

'Hm,' said Mr Trinity, 'let's hope Master Remlin has been successful on his journey to the Ice People!' Mr Trinity took out the Crystal Globe from his cloak and placed it on the ground. A white mist appeared which turned into flakes of snow. Everyone leant forward and looked into the crystal. There was Master Remlin on his white horse as he struggled through a blizzard. In the distance you could see a mountain. Master Remlin started to get closer and, as he struggled on, a door appeared in the side of the mountain and slowly opened inwards. There, standing in the doorway, was a man dressed head to toe in a thick black fur coat and big heavy fur boots. At his side hung a sword and there were daggers tucked into his fur boots. Two men ran from the open door towards Master Remlin and took the reins of his horse and led him through the open door into the mountain. As the door closed, all you could see was the snow swirling round and round in the wind. The mist came back and everything disappeared.

'Well,' said Mr Trinity, 'at least he has reached the end of his journey! He'll be quite safe. Let's hope everything goes all right and he persuades them to join us. They're fearsome warriors, the Ice People.' With that Mr Trinity picked up the Globe and put it back in his cloak. 'Come,' said Mr Trinity, 'let's move'.

All the leaders got up and headed for their soldiers who were by this time ready for the day's march to the final campsite.

Later that day, as I rode along on a horse I had been given by Poppy One, Fairy Nough flew up to me and sat down facing me on the horse's mane.

'John,' she said, 'how are you?'

'I thought you had fallen out with me,' I said. 'Did I upset you?'

'Oh no!' she said in her squeaky voice. 'I've just been busy with my father . . . family business, you know. By the way, do you still have the glass marble my father gave you?'

'Yes,' I replied. 'Why, do you want it back?;

'Oh no, but please take care of it and don't lose it! You will need it if things don't go well tomorrow. I will tell you what to do with it when the time arrives.' Before I could ask her what she meant, off she flew back to her father. *Ah well*, I thought, *I will just have to wait*. I took the marble from my pocket and turned it over in my hand, rubbing my fingers over the smooth surface and wondering what possible use it could be to me or indeed anyone at all. I took one more look at it and put it back safely in my pocket.

Suddenly I heard a noise behind me and up galloped General Dylantos. He came alongside Mr Trinity and informed him that were we are being followed.

'I know!' Mr Trinity replied. 'They've been following us for days . . . It's the Cannibals.'

A lump came into my throat and I gulped hard. I did not like the sound of that. 'Don't worry,' said Mr Trinity, glancing at me. 'It's not *us* they're after. They want rich pickings from the battle tomorrow!' General Dylantos looked pleased. 'When we settle for the night I'll take some men back and talk to Hipictu, the leader, and make him an offer he can't refuse.' With those final words, he turned and galloped away.

We had reached our final destination, our last campsite. Everyone dismounted. Soldiers were running around setting up campfires. Honitos and the Sondron men gathered the wagons in a large semi-circle behind us as a barricade in case anyone tried to attack from the rear by surprise. We were aware that the Cannibals were behind us and we still didn't really know whether they would be friend or foe. General Dylantos was going to find out this evening.

Everyone had gone about their duties as quickly and as silently as they could. The food was cooking and the guards posted round the perimeter.

'Come, boys,' Mr Trinity said. 'I want to show you the battlefield.'

We strode forward until we saw far below us thousands upon thousands of campfires – the enemy army. We were on the top edge of a long steep slope that ran along the edge of the desert. The slope was covered in large boulders, some piled on top of each other. All of a sudden it went dark. The only light came from the moon in the sky and the campfires of Dr Zaker's and Kaunn's army.

In the blackness, the enormity of the army below became alarmingly clear. We headed back to our campfire deep in thought. Mr Trinity sat down and looked at everybody through the flames of the fire.

'Well, ladies and gentlemen, here we are at last! Tomorrow is the big day and we can't give up now.'

Everyone nodded in approval. 'I've had a look at the land below us. In front of us is a steep slope strewn with boulders that leads into a valley. At the end of the valley is a large open space where Dr Zaker is camped with his men . . . There must be at least twenty thousand of them. General Dylantos is going to see the Cannibals, who have been following us for some days. If we can get them to fight alongside us, it will help enormously . . . though they may be here just for the rich pickings.' I swallowed hard, I did not fancy ending up in some cannibal's cooking pot.

Mr Trinity took out the Crystal Globe and placed his hands over it. Everyone waited with apprehension as the mist inside slowly cleared. Master Remlin was on his white horse moving slowly through the snow, his long white hair sticking to the sides of his face from the wet snow. As the mist cleared some more, much to our delight there were the Ice People following Master Remlin, six abreast, row after row. Mr Trinity began to count as they marched past – one, two, three, four thousand men.

Everyone let out a roar! Mr Trinity picked up the Globe and put it back in his cloak. My heart began to beat faster and a feeling of elation came over me. All those soldiers, their uniforms made of fur, each carrying a long lance and a sword tucked in their belts, their silver helmets glinting in the morning sunlight.

Mr Trinity spoke again. 'Don't get carried away by what you've seen. We have to hope he arrives in time! We will wait for as long as possible before we attack, to give Master Remlin more time to reach us.' Everyone nodded.

General Dylantos said, 'I think it's time I went and spoke to Hipictu. Would you like to come along, young John?' I looked at the General. Surely he was joking? But he was serious. I thought for a minute.

'Yes,' I said at last. 'I have to face up to my fears. Anyway I'm only small, not much meat on me for them to eat!'

'Good,' said General Dylantos. 'Let's go!' I got up from my seat beside the warm fire and headed off towards General Dylantos's horse. We climbed up with me sitting in front of him. We headed off, taking four of his best warriors with us, into the dark night where a single fire blazed into the night sky. Nearer and nearer we got until we were about two hundred yards from the campfire.

All I could make out in the firelight was the Cannibals moving about around the fire. Their chalky bodies were poking at something over a spit on the open fire.

General Dylantos shouted: 'Hipictu, Hipictu, it is I, General Dylantos. Can we speak?'

Everything remained silent. Not a sound came from out of the camp. General Dylantos shouted again and then out of the darkness appeared the pygmy chief with four men, almost upon us. We had not seen any movement at all, and yet suddenly there they were in front of us. They had washed the chalky substance from their bodies so as not to be seen in the dark. One of them stepped forward – it was Hipictu. He had removed all his gold jewellery and stood before us in only his loincloth and headdress of feathers.

General Dylantos started to speak using sign language to be understood. Hipictu kept nodding and making hand signs back to the General. General Dylantos turned to me. 'He has invited us back to his camp to talk. We've come this far; we may as well see what he has to say back at his camp.'

Hipictu turned on his heels and General Dylantos and I followed to the Cannibals' campfire where we dismounted and were invited to a seat beside the fire. The other Cannibals were sharpening their knives on stones beside the fire. They looked menacing with their chalky bodies. I looked at the spit on the open fire and felt sick to my stomach. It was one of those creatures that we had encountered the day before in the long grass. A number of them must have got away because, besides the one that was roasting over the fire, there was at least six more trussed up alive just close by. Their eyes were wide with fear. I just kept quiet and looked around while General Dylantos and Hipictu continued to speak in sign language.

After an hour of talking they must have come to some sort of agreement, for General Dylantos suddenly nodded his head and smiled. Hipictu clapped his hands and at once, from out of nowhere, hundreds of pygmies appeared from the scrub. Each one carried a knife in their left hand and a small blowpipe in the other, together with a pouch of small arrows at their waist. Hipictu reached out, took General Dylantos's hand, shook it and smiled.

'Come on, young John. Look's like we've been successful!'

We mounted our horses and headed back towards our camp.

*

Back at the camp everyone was talking tactics. I was too tired by now to listen and I joined Sutherland, who had already gone to sleep. *Things are going well*, I thought, as I fell into oblivion.

I woke in the middle of the night. Everywhere was quiet and nothing stirred. There was just the noise of the fire crackling. Then out of the corner of my eye I saw a movement in the darkness. I caught its shadow in the firelight – it was Honitos. Strangely, though, he no longer shuffled but moved quite lithely on his thin scrawny legs. He moved towards Mr Trinity, who was lying on the ground, seemingly asleep. As Honitos got closer, he quickly took a knife from his belt and lunged at Mr Trinity. I shouted out a warning but already Mr Trinity had raised his hand and grabbed Honitos by the throat. It was over in seconds. Honitos lay on the ground still.

'He's not dead,' said Mr Trinity, 'just – shall we say? – asleep.'

Mr Trinity asked me to go and fetch Christinos, and I jumped up and ran as fast as my legs would carry me. I found her sleeping with her bodyguards. 'Come quickly, my Lady!' I said to her. 'It's Mr Trinity. He's been attacked by Honitos!'

Christinos gathered four of her warriors and raced back towards Mr Trinity, withdrawing her sword as she ran. She reached the campfire slightly out of breath. She looked down at Honitos lying prone on the ground, not moving. She stared at Mr Trinity, eyes wide in horror.

'What have you done, Mr Trinity?' she cried angrily, misunderstanding the situation.

Poppy One spoke up. 'He tried to attack Mr Trinity. Don't know why!' he said.

'Is this true?' Christinos asked Mr Trinity.

Mr Trinity nodded.

Christinos walked up to Honitos and kicked him in his ribs. 'Wake up! wake up!' she commanded.

Mr Trinity reached out and took hold of her arm gently in his long bony fingers. 'Stop!' he said. 'I knew he was going to attack me as soon as we came to your camp. Show her how I knew, John,' he said.

I pulled the small Golden Heart from my pocket and gave it to Mr Trinity. Mr Trinity showed it to Christinos. The heart gave off a golden glow as she touched it with her hand.

'Now watch,' said Mr Trinity, and slowly took the Heart away and placed it on the now waking Honitos. Almost at once the light faded. Christinos looked on in amazement as Mr Trinity explained how the Heart worked. He gave it back to me and I put it back in my inside pocket. By this time Honitos had come completely round and was trying to raise himself from the ground. Christinos stopped him by placing her foot on his scrawny throat and holding her sword to his chest. She shouted to Judithos, who came across with two of her soldiers. 'Take him away! Don't let him out of your sight . . . I will deal with him later.' The two soldiers dragged the hepless Honitos away, his feet scraping the ground as he went.

Christinos put her sword back in its scabbard and looked at Mr Trinity. 'I'm sorry for doubting you. Can you forgive me, Mr Trinity?'

He looked at her with a twinkle in his eye and touched her on the arm with his long bony fingers. 'There's nothing to forgive,' he said, smiling.

He let go of her arm and she smiled back.

'I will see you in the morning then!' She turned away and headed for her campfire. She was probably going to get the truth out of Honitos – why he did what he tried to do.

*

Once again I lay down and tried to sleep, drifting in and out of troubled dreams. My mind was in turmoil thinking that something else was going to happen that night. I do not think I had been asleep for very long when what sounded like an alarm clock woke me up. I rubbed my eyes and opened them wide. One of Christinos's soldiers was ringing the bell that stood in the middle of the camp. Sutherland and I jumped up and looked around. The soldiers from every tribe were busy setting up defensive positions to surround us. General Giedroyc's men were patrolling overhead, their silver uniforms just catching the earliest rays of the dawn. Their crossbows at the ready, they were flying in a diamond formation above us. We ran towards Mr Trinity at great speed, running over the flat sand and kicking small stones as we went. But Mr Trinity did not seem at all moved by the commotion that was going on all around us. We buried our heads under his black cloak. Much to our shame, Mr Trinity laughed out loud. 'Come, come out from under there, boys. It's only a prac-tice. You never know so it's is best to be prepared!'

Sutherland and I peered out from under the cloak to see the two Poppies grinning from ear to ear.

'It's OK boys,' they said in unison. 'Nothing to be afraid of . . . yet.' They smiled and shook their heads.

The bell stopped ringing General Giedroyc's men began to land and everyone started to go back to doing their normal duties. Sutherland and I gave a sigh of relief, but were a little shamefaced all the same. How would we behave when the real battle came?

19

Over breakfast, everyone was arguing about strategy. Everyone knew best of course . . . Perhaps there were just *too* many generals. General Dylantos interrupted.

'Look,' he said. Everyone's eyes turned to the edge of the camp and there stood the leader of the Cannibals, Hipictu. His body was covered in white chalk, his head adorned with a headdress of multicoloured feathers, and his neck hung with gold jewellery. The bone in his nose was bleached lily white and large earrings hung from each of his earlobes. Six warriors accompanied him. Each carried a small bow and a small blowpipe. General Dylantos got up and headed towards the Cannibal chief. On reaching him, he raised his left hand in some sort of greeting. After a few moments, he gestured to Hipictu and his men to come forward to where we were all sitting around the campfire. They reached the campfire and General Dylantos asked them to sit. The warriors sat down cross-legged and put their bows on the ground. They stared around the campfire, looking everyone up and down. General Dylantos turned to Mr Trinity.

'He's prepared to help us but he wants to know what's in it for him. He said he won't do it for nothing.'

Mr Trinity nodded his head and took out the Crystal Globe. Into view came Dr Zaker and his grotesque army. They were shouting his name and thrusting their weapons into the air. Hipictu recoiled, his eyes staring wide. He could not understand the magic of the Crystal Globe. The Globe began to mist over and Dr Zaker and his army disappeared from view. Mr Trinity picked up the Globe and put it back in his cloak. He turned to General Dylantos. 'Tell him he can have any prisoners that are left for himself and his people.'

I gulped at the thought of those evil creatures roasting over an open fire, but quickly dismissed my scruples. They were evil, just evil, like Dr Zaker and Kaunn. Hipictu communicated with General Dylantos and nodded and smiled. General Dylantos turned to Mr Trinity. 'That's fine, but he wants something on account.'

Everyone looked at each other in horror. We did not have any prisoners. Suddenly Christinos snapped her fingers and three of her warriors came running forward. They bent down and she whispered in their ears. They turned round and ran off. A few minutes later they came back dragging Honitos behind them, his scrawny body kicking up dust.

Christinos pointed at Honitos and said, 'Will he do?'

Hipictu strode forward and began to feel the scrawny body of Honitos, poking him and squeezing his arms and legs like a piece of meat at market. I felt sick to my stomach. Surely Mr Trinity would not allow this to happen. I know he was a traitor but surely he didn't deserve this.

Reading my thoughts, Mr Trinity put his hand on my shoulder, 'I don't want to do this . . . no one does . . . but we do need the Cannibals' help. You understand, don't you?'

Hipictu signed to General Dylantos, who translated. 'Bit scrawny . . . not much meat but he'll do until the morning when they would be able to take their pick.'

Honitos started to scream.

Hipictu raised his arm and gave Honitos a blow to the

side of the temple. Instantly he dropped like a stone and lay lifeless on the ground. Two of the Cannibals tied some rope round his ankles and began to drag his lifeless body back to their camp.

Hipictu turned to General Dylantos, raised his left hand in salute and followed his men. Everyone sat in stunned silence not saying a word, just trying to take it all in and trying to understand why.

The daylight hours were spent in discussing tactics and preparing. It had been decided that a night-time attack was best. The main thrust of the strategy was to draw Dr Zaker and his army into the valley. Some of the troops would be transported by air to land behind Dr Zaker's lines; others would attack from the sides of the valley.

Everyone was now hastily going about their business. Some were sharpening their swords and spears; others checking their crossbows. By now, the sun was disappearing over the horizon and the darkness descended like some thick blanket. You could just see the shadows of the troops as they waited for the order to proceed to their positions and make ready for the battle that was to happen just before daybreak. 'The element of surprise is what we need,' said Mr Trinity. 'That gives us a fighting chance!' Poppy One and Two went round telling everyone to douse the campfires. One by one, the fires vanished, plunging the whole camp into darkness. Even the moon and stars seemed to have been extinguished.

Soon it was time for King Gandelin and his men to fly off in their bird-powered baskets. King Gandelin got in the first one and then Generals Travin and Rol got in the two rear baskets. The lead soldier in every basket lit a small torch and waved it to and fro above his head. Out of the black night came King Gandelin's Migasaurous followed by the smaller Synisaurouses. The flap of their wings filled the air, making a whistling noise like the wind as it blows through the trees. As each bird came down, it picked up a basket and flew off again until all the baskets were in the air. They passed above us like some great big black rain cloud above our heads. Suddenly they were gone and silence fell over the camp once again.

Christinos and Judithos came up to Mr Trinity they didn't look happy. 'I thought we were going with King Gandelin,' Christinos said in an angry voice.

'I'm sorry,' said Mr Trinity, 'but we wouldn't have time to make two trips. In any case, I think you'll be much more useful here. You can help draw Dr Zaker's forces into the valley where everyone else will be waiting.

The women calmed down and accepted his apology.

The night was passing quickly and yet there was so much still to do. Soon, though, everyone was ready to take up their positions. Christinos and Judithos mounted their horses; they had already armed the Sondron men with weapons. King Ronough had split his soldiers into two. The archers were positioned on the top of the hill while the remainder, led by himself, joined Christinos and Judithos and proceeded down the hill to the valley floor below. General Dylantos had already taken his archers to either side of the valley. Alcyoneus and Enceladus were stationed with their men among the boulders that scattered the hillside. General Giedroyc with his Tyrocdiles waited patiently with his men for the signal to go. But where was Hipictu and his Cannibal warriors? Mr Trinity took out the Crystal Globe and began to peer into its mists. There were King Gandelin's men marching towards Dr Zaker's army. The great Synisaurouses and Migasaurous were on their way back . . . but it showed him little else. Mr Trinity put the Globe back in his cloak.

'Come, boys,' he said. 'Come with me.'

Taking us by the hand, he took Sutherland and me to a

large semi-circle of rocks and told us to hide. Alycyoneus and Enceladus picked up a large boulder and placed it in front of the entrance. We could see everything going on outside, but we were perfectly safe . . . for the moment. 'Stay there,' Mr Trinity said, 'and don't move! I will come for you when it's all over.'

It was almost dawn. Bolts of lightning began to appear in the distance and then suddenly a crack of the thunder burst across the valley like some giant bellowing. Mr Trinity gave the signal, and Christinos, Judithos and King Ronough with their soldiers began to move along the valley floor, there horses kicking up the dry dust and making a cloud as they went.

20

Suddenly the heavens opened and torrential rain fell on the advancing horsemen and women. Two hundred yards in front were the Silvienes, snarling and showing their razor-sharp teeth, their bloodshot eyes peering out of their black leather helmets. There must have been at least five thousand of them! They were chanting and banging their spears onto the now soaking-wet ground.

There was no sign of either Dr Zaker or Kaunn. The torrential rain continued to fall, making the Silvienes' leather uniforms glisten ominously. The enemy still did not move but just kept on banging their spears onto the ground. Then suddenly, without warning, the vulture-like Angasaurouses appeared in air, at least two hundred of them. They flew over Christinos and Judithos and began to let loose their barbed arrows, taking our troops by surprise. Christinos, Judithos and King Ronough along with their troops retreated along the valley floor to the safety of the boulders, leaving their dead or wounded soldiers lying on the sodden ground. Where were King Gandelin's Synisaurouses?

Still the Silvienes remained motionless. Mr Trinity gave General Giedroyc the signal. His men took to the air and started to pick off the Angasaurouses one by one. They were helpless. They could not get their bows loaded quickly enough as General Giedroyc's men fired arrow after arrow into their hideous fleshy bodies. With each piercing arrow that went into them, they let out an almighty scream that sent shivers down my spine. Their bodies began to fall to the valley floor, each one making a sickening thud as it hit the ground. And, as each one fell, Christinos and the Sondron warriors ran forward and severed their heads from their wriggling bodies. The wet valley floor turned red with the blood of the slain. The Angasaurouses then began to retreat, that is what was left of them.

Next out of the dark clouds came King Gandelin's Synisaurouses and their riders who let fly their arrows at the remaining Angasaurouses. The arrows pierced right through their bodies and brought them to the ground until not one remained in the sky. King Gandelin's birds now turned their attention to the Silvienes on the ground along with General Giedroyc's Tyrocdiles.

They let fly every arrow they had. It was like black rain. The Silvienes began to retreat, leaving the wet earth scattered with the broken bodies of their comrades. There was still no sign of Dr Zaker and Kaunn; they hadn't taken the bait. Mr Trinity had won the first round, as they say, but what now? That had been just a small force; Dr Zaker had a lot more men. What would he do next? They had to be able to draw him into the valley if they stood any chance of success.

Mr Trinity took the Crystal Globe once more from his cloak and rubbed it gently. The mist began to clear and, low and behold, there were King Gandelin's troops lined up at the rear of Dr Zaker who sat astride his large black horse. In his left hand Dr Zaker held a short stabbing sword and in his right was his black shield emblazoned with the skull and crossbones. King Gandelin's troops would not stand a chance against all those Silvienes – two thousand against ten thousand. King Gandelin started to charge towards Dr Zaker, their swords drawn at the ready. The rain kept on coming down, making pools of water on the ground. King Gandelin's archers, too, were busy, raining arrow after arrow on the enemy army. Creatures fell on every side, but Dr Zaker seemed immune.

Mr Trinity summoned Christinos and showed her the battle.

'Quickly, attack him and draw his troops into the valley!' he ordered.

Christinos mounted her horse and along with Judithos and the rest of her warriors started to gallop along the valley floor, waving their swords above their heads. Into the Silvienes they rode, slashing cutting and stabbing with their short swords. Then suddenly, Christinos sounded the retreat and led her troops back towards the entrance of the valley. The Sllvienes sensed victory and, breaking rank, started to run after Christinos and her warriors. Dr Zaker, on his great black steed, was dismayed and started to ride along the front of his warriors, trying to rally them into one big block.

They did not have much time, for now King Gandelin's men were upon them, shouting and screaming at the top of their voices. You could hear the sound of metal upon metal as they slashed at each other with their short swords and daggers. King Gandelin and his men could not make much headway; the Silvienes were too many and stronger than King Gandelin's men. Where was Master Remlin and the Ice People? King Gandelin's men began to fall back slowly under the superior forces of Dr Zaker.

Suddenly in the distance, coming out of the rain and lightning, *was* Master Remlin and the Ice People. Master Remlin on his white horse, his blue robe flowing behind him in the wind, headed straight for Dr Zaker. He held his sword straight out in front of him, his horse kicking up mud as it galloped over the plain making its white legs black with dirt. The Ice People rushed in with their big axes, cutting and chopping into the Silvienes.

Now King Ronough signalled to his archers overlooking

the valley floor to make ready. The Silvienes that had followed Christinos and Judithos stopped in their tracks, realising it was a trap and that the only way out was back. They turned on their clawed feet and began to run back towards the rest of Dr Zaker's and Kaunn's forces. Too late! King Ronough signalled to his archers again and they let fly their arrows down into the valley, like a large black thunderous cloud. The arrows pierced the Silvienes' bodies, bringing hundreds down onto the valley floor. Dozens after dozens fell, their half-human, half-bird heads sinking into the mud. Some lay still and others tried to move and crawl. Their screams echoed around the valley like banshees screaming in the night. In the distance, you could see Dr Zaker trying to rally the Tainos but they now turned and fled – they knew they could not win.

Dr Zaker turned his great black horse and headed away from Master Remlin, climbing the hill at the foot of the valley. He reached the top and stood on the flat plain signalling to his men to follow. Soon Dr Zaker and a few hundred of his men began to advance across the hill, trying to get round the back of Mr Trinity in a flanking movement. It was a clever move.

But, at that moment, from out of nowhere came Hipictu and his Cannibal warriors. They streamed down onto the valley floor, waving their spears and shouting at the top of their voices. Soon a fierce and confused battle raged. The sound of weapon against weapon and scream upon scream filled the air as the two armies clashed like a swarm of locusts. It was all down to brute strength and tactics. Dr Zaker continued his advance along the top of the hill with his few hundred men.

Mr Trinity summoned Alcyoneus and ordered him to take his men along with the remainder of Christinos's troops and King Ronough's archers to engage Dr Zaker and the rest of his Silvienes.

Dr Zaker and his few hundred Silviene troops had reached the flat plain at the top of the hill and were beginning to advance along it towards the giant warriors of the Scordisi. By now Mr Trinity had been joined by Master Remlin, who was now directing the battle that raged all around us.

'We are losing too many men!' said Master Remlin. 'We have to do something.'

Fairy Nough flew up to me. 'Give me the glass marble! Quickly!' she said in a hurried voice. I took the marble from my pocket and gave it to her. She took it in her tiny hand and flew to Mr Trinity and Master Remlin. She handed Mr Trinity the marble and began to explain what to do.

Mr Trinity summoned General Giedroyc and told him to get his men away from the centre of the battle, where they had been flying overhead, picking off the Silvienes on the ground with their crossbows. Meanwhile, Master Remlin and Christinos galloped round towards Alcyoneus and his giants and told them not to advance any further. General Dylantos gave a pre-arranged signal and all the troops on the ground began to retreat to where they had come from. The Silvienes left on the valley floor stopped and began to make a defensive ring. The Ice People, too, had retreated back to the opening of the valley.

The rain was coming down in torrents; it was like a waterfall, soaking everyone, and everything. The drops were bouncing off the ground like small pebbles. There was silence except for the sound of thunder and the crackle of the lightning as it pierced the air. The storm was now right above us. The Silvienes on the valley floor just stood there in silence, looking up into the air.

'Throw the marble into the air now!' Fairy Nough told Mr Trinity.

Mr Trinity took the marble in his right hand and threw it into the air high above the Silvienes. As it left the palm of his hand it began to grow larger and larger until it was about the size of a hot-air balloon. Suddenly a bolt of lightning connected to the large sphere of glass and shattered it, into thousands of pieces. Slivers of glass as sharp as a sword began to fall upon the Silvienes below, piercing their bodies. They began to fall like ninepins in a bowling alley. Everyone began to cheer, but it was not over yet. Not all of them had fallen.

Mr Trinity signalled to Enceladus to start the advance with the rest of the Scordisi giants. They pushed on the large boulders, their huge arms and bulging biceps straining to the limit to move them. One by one, the boulders started to roll down the hill, quickly followed by the giants.

The Silvienes panicked and began to run back towards the Ice People and King Gandelin's men. They were running as fast as they could on their short stubby legs. Their clawed feet were sticking in the mud on the valley floor, but it was too late! The boulders reached them, crushing their bodies and snapping their backs like twigs.

Mr Trinity now gave the signal for King Gandelin and the Ice People to attack once more. The Silvienes had nowhere to run and were quickly cut to pieces; their screams echoing round the valley floor and then fading to nothing. There was a deathly silence. I looked down at the scene that lay before me, a mass of broken and dying bodies, the Silvienes and Mr Trinity's warriors lying side by side. However, it still wasn't over even yet. There was Dr Zaker and Kaunn to deal with.

Dr Zaker was steadily advancing as he tried to come up on our rear flank. However, Christinos and her soldiers started to outflank Dr Zaker on the right, while Alcyoneus and Enceladus advanced from the front. It was an awesome sight, these giants advancing like tall oak trees, waving their clubs and swords like branches swaying in the wind. Out of the corner of my eye, I saw the two Poppies galloping towards Dr Zaker. They bent forward in the saddles of their horses, swords straight out in front of them like a cavalry charge in the movies.

The giants collided with the enemy, hitting with their clubs and chopping at them with huge axes. They were cutting them down as if they were sheaves of wheat in a wheat field. The Silvienes were no match for the giant Scordisi warriors. Those that were lying wounded or in their final death throes were savaged by the two giant dogs who ripped away the flesh from their bones, Christinos and Judithos rode valiantly into the carnage, despatching many a Silviene with their short swords and daggers. Oh, revenge was sweet!

By now the two Poppies had reached Dr Zaker on his jet-black horse. His shield was in his left hand and his huge sword in his right hand. He used his skull-and-crossbones shield to parry away the shower of crossbow bolts that rained down on him. He seemed invincible. The brothers were determined to gain revenge for what he had put them through all those years ago. They were not going to let someone else take away that sweet moment from them; they had waited a long time for this moment. Mr Trinity signalled to General Giedroyc to call off his Tyrocdiles. He knew what this meant to the two Poppies.

The Poppies had now engaged their prey. Dr Zaker fended off blow after blow with his shield. One of the Poppies slashed at Dr Zaker's body with his sword, cutting through his black uniform that was now stained with blood. He tried to fight them off with the huge sword he held in his right hand, but, as he attacked, the other Poppy attacked him from the rear, cutting deep into his torso. Dr Zaker tried to turn his huge black steed so that he could retreat, but his horse stumbled on the wet ground and fell. Dr Zaker was thrown into the mud. He tried to get up but already one of the Poppies pinned him to the ground with his sword.

The two brothers dismounted and strode over to Dr

Zaker, the rain dripping off their large black beards. They stood over Dr Zaker as he lay defenceless in the mud. Once more he tried to get up from the rain-sodden ground but simultaneously both the Poppies buried their sword deep into Dr Zaker's chest. He let out a scream and fell back. He was silent.

Everything fell silent. There was just the sound of the rain falling onto the ground and the noise of thunder as it disappeared in the distance. Dr Zaker was dead but where was Kaunn? After all, he was the real power behind their affair. Dr Zaker had been little more than a puppet. In our 'cave', I shook Sutherland by the shoulders. He was standing beside me, still with his hands over his ears and his eyes tight shut. He did not take any notice of me, so I tried to prise away his left hand from his ear. 'It's all over now! it's finished! You can look now,' I said.

Slowly he opened his eyes and surveyed the battlefield in front of us. A tear began to roll down his cheek and he started to cry, which in turn set me off crying also. After all, we had been through so much together.

Now Mr Trinity came towards us; and pulled us gently to his side.

'Come on, boys, it's all over! We've won.' The softness of his voice and the warmth of his cloak calmed our fears and our tears were quelled.

I looked around at the battlefield with the dead of both sides lying in the rain-soaked valley. The rain had stopped; there was no more lightning or thunder. The dark clouds had disappeared and the sun started to dry out the rain puddles, leaving a misty haze above the valley floor. We were now in bright sunlight.

Suddenly Sutherland shouted, 'Look, look!'

Mr Trinity turned to where Sutherland was pointing. It was Kaunn. He had taken Dr Zaker's horse. 'We will meet again, Trinity. This isn't over yet.' He let out a loud screeching laugh, the great black horse reared up, turned and then galloped away into the distance. General Giedroyc offered to pursue him but Mr Trinity refused. 'We will find him one day. He can't hide for ever. For now, let us cremate our dead. As for the Silvienes, leave them for the Cannibals. They deserve their taste of victory.'

Everyone went down into the valley and began to remove their dead warriors. They placed them in piles according to their tribe – the Sondrons, the Gawen peoples, the fairies, the Volsci people and even some giants. There was not one tribe that was without its war dead.

At last the sun began to set over the horizon and night seemed like a gift as it threw its mantle over the horrors of the battlefield. One by one, the funeral pyres were lit and one by one they slowly burst into flames. Mr Trinity looked on with great sorrow in his eyes. 'Come, boys, it's time to rest.' We headed for a campfire and Sutherland and I sat down against a large boulder either side of Mr Trinity. I looked around at all the leaders of the tribes – King Gandelin; King Ronough with Fairy Nough at his side; General Giedroyc of the Tyrocdiles; General Dylantos of the Gawen; Christinos and Judithos; Alcyoneus and Enceladus . . . and of course the two Poppies. One by one, each leader rose from the campfire and headed towards their warriors. Now there was only Mr Trinity, the two Poppies, Master Remlin and Fairy Nough. Fairy Nough sat down beside me and took my hand in her tiny hand.

'It has been a pleasure to know you, John. I wish you a safe journey home, and maybe, one day, we will meet again . . . I will miss you.' She leant over, kissed me on each cheek and was then gone in a flash. Only her tiny voice still rang in my ear: 'Goodbye! Goodbye till the next time!'

Master Remlin now started to speak.

'Boys, boys,' he said, 'it's time to rest. It's a long way home for you both.'

He pointed towards a large boulder and told us to sleep there. We stumbled towards it, looking forward to our night's rest. Before we slept we looked out at the funeral pyres burning in the night sky, feeling both sorrow and joy. Mr Trinity came over and told us to sleep, his voice so gentle and kind. He put his hands over our eyes.

'Sleep now for tomorrow will soon be here,' he said, and through the gaps between his long bony fingers I saw an orange mist come out from his mouth, the same orange mist that had come from the Crystal Globe I had seen him breathe in a few days before. It surrounded us and I felt my eyes grow heavy.

'Sleep now, boys . . .'

21

I awoke the next morning with what sounded like a bell ringing and a woman's voice shouting in a high-pitched tone. 'Up, up! Come on! Up! Breakfast in an hour.' I rubbed my eyes and opened them slowly. I was back in my own bed in the dormitory. I looked across next to me and there was Sutherland muttering to himself like he always did. I leant over and shook him by the shoulders.

'Sutherland, Sutherland!' I said. 'We're back in our beds!'

'I know, I know! Been here all night.' came the caustic reply.

'Don't you remember?' I said.

'Remember what?'

I began to doubt the whole thing myself. Had it been all a dream?

Mrs Pickersgill came into the dorm. 'Come on, boys. Breakfast in an hour. Get ready and don't dawdle!'

At breakfast I ate greedily as if I had not had a good meal for quite some time. After I had finished I got up, headed for the schoolroom and took my place at my desk alongside Sutherland. Everyone was talking until Mrs Pickersgill came to the front of the class. 'Boys, boys,' she said, 'we have a new teacher for you today.'

I heard a cloak swishing across the wooden floor and a dark figure walked past me with an eerie presence. I hardly dared look.

'Now, boys, I want you to meet Mr Trinity, your new teacher.'

I froze, I just sat there head down, buried in my book. I did not dare look up until a thin hand with long bony fingers removed the book from underneath my nose and took it away.

'Good morning!' a voice said in a calm soothing way. 'My name is Mr Trinity.'

I slowly raised my head and looked up and there he was, just as he had been in my dream.

Mr Trinity looked down at me with those blue piercing eyes that shone out of his thin gaunt face.

'Good morning, John,' he said with a twinkle in his eye.